LOST WHISPERS

"a literary mystery"

By Edward Casey Michaels

ISBN 978-1-4507-1522-5

Printed in the United States of America by Gage Printing Company
220 Buckner Drive, Battle Creek, Michigan 49037
First Edition, First Printing, April 2010

PROLOGUE

lost whispers is the story of a young man taking a brief spring vacation in michigan's upper peninsula in order to investigate his family's grandparents. he is also going to try and shake off the recent michigan winter and get the snow and icy temperatures out of his system.

while traveling he discovers the mystery of a long forgotten poet t. kilgore splake. in pursuing his past personal history the young man finds an unanswered question about one of his relatives. besides the mystery of the lost poet splake and the question of what happened to luigi meneguzzo's son, the adventure ends with a possible new romance for the author.

the reader of *lost whispers* should realize that the story is not based on true facts about actual people and events. however, since the author knows many of the central characters in the *lost whispers* drama, he has chosen to remain anonymous. there is no edward casey michaels. these are the first names of my three children, edward (teddy) stephen, casey gillian, and michael brendan. the geographic locations in *lost whispers* are all accurate upper peninsula places. the names of many of the people "teddy" michaels meets during his travels range from real yoopers to others whose identities have been changed.

"your vision will become clear only when you look into your heart . . . who looks outside, dreams. who looks inside, awakens."

carl gustave jung

1

"one day while studying a (william butler) yeats poem i decided to write poetry for the rest of my life. i recognized that a single short poem has room for history, music, psychology, religious thought, mood, occult speculation, character, and events of one's own life."

robert bly

"epiphany: was the sudden 'revelation of the whatness of a thing,' the moment when the soul of the commonest object...seems to us radiant."

james joyce

"seeming utterly fragile and vulnerable, the silhouette pulsed almost imperceptibly with the beating of her heart or the motions of her inner heart, as if she were whispering soundless words to the darkness."

haruki murakami

it was early morning and the battle creek city limits sign was in my rearview mirror. with a tank full of petrol and the humming tranny horses, i knew i should make the mackinaw bridge before high noon.

i had survived the michigan "season of long white" with dark days, snow, ice and arctic temperatures. a "cabin fever" vacation from my position as "placement officer" at the kellogg company in battle creek, michigan, seemed like an excellent idea. in a very short time many new college graduates would be sending me their applications and hoping for a job interview. early in june i would be making the employment choices for new hires in the "cereal city."

the vacation traveling itinerary was to drive to iron mountain in michigan's upper peninsula. with my thirtieth birthday coming up soon i had suddenly developed an interest in just who my grandmother and grandfather were. i wanted to visit their grave sites to pay my respects. also, i wanted to see what i could find out about their lives in iron mountain years ago.

my grandfather, luigi meneguzzo, had been a struggling farmer in castelgomberto, italy, where he fell in love and married carissima branz. luigi then immigrated to the united states and found a job at the chapin iron mine in iron mountain, michigan. he saved his earnings and after three years of working the mines he sent funds for carrissima and his young daughter, theresa, to join him.

there would be no stopping for something to drink or eat during the highway miles. the artful dodger was stocked with a twelve-pack of diet coke, some german black pumpernickel bread, a fat wedge of aged jarlsberg, and several thick slices of prime braunschweiger.

winter was still fading into spring, so i packed some extra sweaters for any cool temperatures in the upper peninsula. i decided to leave my camera at home but i packed the laptop computer just in case i might need it.

the divided interstate highway was my quickest route to u.s. 69. i avoided driving in downtown lansing and had a straight shot north to the mackinaw bridge and michigan's upper peninsula.

north of st. johns, the sky turned into light gray shadows of the morning's early dawn. suddenly i felt free of battle creek, the job, and my current life responsibilities. north of mount pleasant and the exit for central michigan university, the thickly forested land had fewer family farming operations.

with the increase in wilderness, occasionally i would see a tent camper or small house trailer on a remote parcel of land. i thought it sad that people would think of this location as the exciting far north filled with hunting, fishing and camping adventures. if one really wanted to escape metropolitan areas and couldn't move to alaska or canada, why not a remote vacation homestead in the upper peninsula?

with the speedometer locked in at 70 miles-per-hour, i remembered a long since past greyhound bus trip from battle creek to marquette in the upper peninsula. while driving home from a winter weekend at the "ice carnival" at michigan technological university in houghton my ford bronco "ate a piston."

choosing not to buy a used car that could possibly be in worse shape than my ford, i negotiated the installation of a "short block" engine replacement in my bronco. then i rented a car, returned to battle creek, and after the christmas holiday i was riding the "square wheels" north to get my repaired car. between battle creek and marquette, the greyhound stopped at every possible location. indeed, it was a very weary teddy who paid the bill for the new engine in a marquette restaurant then drove back, staying overnight at the terrace motel in munising in order to feel like i was already heading home.

i caught the tall mackinaw bridge stanchions rising in the sky about eleven miles south of mackinaw city and the bridge toll booths. crossing the bridge i noticed a lake freighter moving up lake huron which would soon be sailing under the mackinaw

4

bridge.

with winter - what the yoopers call their season in the long white - over and ice out on the great lakes, the shipping season had already returned. lake superior had the iron ore carrying vessels that filled their holds at the ore docks in duluth, minnesota, and marquette. other lake freighters carried coal, cereals, and cargos to indiana and chicago ports.

i assumed that seeing a great lake boat while crossing the "big mac" was a good omen and that my upper peninsula vacation visit should go well. shipping on the great lakes has always been a fascinating subject for me. i have always dreamed that if i were wealthy and free i would own a cabin outside st. ignace, maybe at gros cap or point aux chenes, and collect the names of freighters that i would capture with my binoculars.

the miles on michigan highway 2 paralleled much of the lake michigan shoreline as i passed through brevort, epoufette, and naubinaway. for some unknown reason i turned north at the highway 2 and 78 junction and continued north.

as i passed through blaney park, i slowed the tranny down to inspect the old buildings. around the turn of the century, blaney park had been a successful logging town and lumbering operation. by 1926, the timbering had expired and the earle family, owners of the wisconsin land and lumber company, tried to make the area a vacation site. there were hiking and horse riding trails, a restaurant, tennis courts and a golf course. the blaney park resort even had their own private air field. after the 1950's, the attitude of vacationers was not to stay at a cabin in blaney park for a week or two, but instead to travel to many different places. while passing through blaney park on my way north to germfask, i saw a man raking the front yard at "celibeth house." i stopped and asked him if there were any future plans for blaney park. without a word he shrugged a negative response.

while slowing down to the 45 miles-per-hour speed limit in the village of germfask, i noticed a bunch of "stuff" sitting on the sidewalk in front of a large two car garage. there were chairs, an old television set on a wooden table, vintage oil paintings and a rusted fat-tire bicycle. suddenly i saw the home-made sign that advertised this as the "yard sale."

curious and also needing an excuse to get out and stretch my legs, i parked at the curbside and met the "yard sale" proprietor, tom pratt. i told him that germfask seemed to be an extremely quiet upper peninsula village. tom explained the interesting history behind the community name of germfask. he told me the town's name came from the initials of the last names of the eight men who had settled the township in 1881. they were john grant, matthew edge, george robinson, thaddeus mead, w.w. french, ezekiel ackley, oscar sheppard, and hezekiah knags. i also learned that the community had been called the "dump," because the lumbermen used to dump their logs into the manistique river to float down to the saw mill in manistique, michigan.

while browsing through some old books in a dusty rotating wire stand in the middle of the "yard sale" i noticed a small thin volume of poetry. the cover of the collection had a faded coffee stain, and its title was *soul whispers*. the poems were written and published by t. kilgore splake, which seemed like a very curious name.

i paid tom the dollar price for the *soul whispers* poetry, wished him a good day, and continued my turning of artful dodger tranny miles north to the village of seney. just a couple miles outside of germfask i came upon the seney national wildlife refuge. i decided to stop, drink a can of diet coke, and read a poem or three from *soul whispers*. i read and reread the splake's "poem for alastor."

poem for alastor

alastar – androgynous half-spirit half man
who lived in the woods and worshipped intellectual
beauty

percy bysshe shelly

hey, will you look at that old guy with the huge gray
beard, man, his skin must be tough as an old alligator
hide, sure takes his time hiking down the road, wonder
where he lives,

you ever met him, what is he really like, where the
hell did he come from,

understand he retired after too many years and students
in some downstate college classroom, lost a wife about the
time, rumors that he was a talented writer, a poet it seems,
but for some reason quit,

now he spends all his time trout fishing, has all the
"topos" between grand marais and melstrand memorized,
stored in his brain, say there's not a rainbow hole or
beaver dam brookie pond he doesn't know about,

april he sets up a camp somewhere and lives off the
trout he catches, vegetables from his garden hidden in
the woods, moving on to new waters, pond or stream
section when the fishing turns poor, lives this way until
the end of october and it really turns cold,

folks think there's an old trailer out near ross lake
where he caches stuff, rice, hooks, line, clearing for a
small garden, place where he leans in during the winter,

every time i see him moseying down the road or
across the plains i get a bit jealous, fresh trout, cooked
rice, spring vegetables, and wild sassafras tea isn't
exactly a crazy way of life, hmm,

but one day he'll have to pick a single trout stream
and become a ghost, waiting to surprise anyone who
discovers his camp

i really liked the poet's image of the hermit-poet-fisherman
living alone in the woods. i did not understand splake's line
changes and the poem's indentations, but i assumed those
techniques came with the wisdom of writing poetry.

my brief pause at the wildlife refuge was suddenly interrupted
by a park ranger who introduced himself as scott fitzgerald. i
replied with a chuckle, "well, at least you are not scott fitzgerald
with an 'f' in front of your name." the ranger did not reply and
i realized splake's verse had spurred me into making the f. scott
fitzgerald reference. ranger scott told me the seney national
wildlife refuge had been established in 1935, for the protection and
production of migratory birds. he said the spring is an excellent
time for "bird watching," with many eagles, ospreys, loons,
and trumpeter swans still on their nests. i declined the ranger's
invitation to stop at the seney wildlife's refuge visitor center, and
his offer of a seven-mile car tour through the wilderness wetlands.

suddenly i realized it was late in the afternoon. i wanted to get
a tank full of petrol in seney then decide what to do next. while
the service-station manager was pumping gallons of lead-free gas
in my car, a seney local pulled up and shouted, "hey, clive, are
you getting ready to sell beer and brats to all of those tourists this
summer who want to find the ghost of ernest hemingway?"

while paying for the gas-fillup, i discovered that the grocery
store-gasoline station owner's name was "cleve," and not "clive."
it seems that his parents had named him after the president "grover
cleveland" many years ago, and the nickname "cleve" managed to
stick.

cleve also told me that ernest hemingway had visited seney
in 1919, to fish the fox river for trout, and to recover from his
world war one wounds. he explained that hemingway in his "nick
adams stories" had changed the name of the fox river in his tale of

camping and fishing to the big two-hearted river. it seems this was done to keep his fishing spot secret, or for the romantic sounds that the big two-hearted river possessed. cleve suggested that i visit the old seney railroad station and museum in the next block where the michigan technological university had established a hemingway exhibition.

after looking over the hemingway display done by michigan technological students, i met a young man packing his rucksack at a picnic table outside. the fellow introduced himself as bruce clark and told me he was a burned-out professor from a college below the bridge. he explained that he planned to spend his entire summer camping on the island in ross lake, up north in the pictured rocks lake superior area, in order to get his head back together.

bruce also told me he had a case of blue ribbon, three dozen nightcrawlers, some home-made cheese made by the mennonites from the seney iga store, and his summer reading library of herman hesse paperbacks. my fast perusal of bruce's ruck-collection revealed: *peter camenzind, beneath the wheel, gertrude, rosshalde, knulp, demian, klingsor's last summer, siddartha, steppenwolf, narcissus and goldmund*, and *the glass bead game*.

i also learned that bruce had fifteen pounds of long-grained brown rice that he would use for cooking ross lake garlic and catfish stews. he explained how the catfish feed at night and he always catches tomorrow's dinner in a short half-hour to forty-five minutes of fishing. bruce also gave me the hesse book *steppenwolf*, explaining that through some bookkeeping mistake his college bookstore order had delivered two copies of this title. i thanked bruce for his spring season kindness and said that i hoped he would have a fantastic summer, returning to the college campus full of fresh energy and excitement.

all of a sudden i felt exhausted. i got a single-bed room at the fox river motel and ate two huge upper peninsula "pasties" while watching the noise on the motel's television set. i leafed through the pages of *steppenwolf* but i was too tired to get involved in the existential tale of discovery by hesse's character harry haller. i did

9

note the interesting references to the "magic theater, entrance not for everybody, for mad men only" which should make for some lively page turning when i have a fresh mind and a more relaxed opportunity to read.

 i found myself clutching the splake book of poems *soul whispers*. after my conversation with cleve and the visit to the seney railroad depot museum, i read the splake poem "fox river odyssey with nick adams."

fox river odyssey with nick adams

tried the question a couple of times in seney, "anyone who still remembers when ernest hemingway jumped out of the boxcar for a fishing trip and made the fox river the big two-hearted of literary fame,"

one spring, cleve, at the mobilgas said "the old SOB probably just came and stayed drunk for a week, slept under the bridge, never wetting a line, then went back to the newspaper and made up his story,"

next spring, cleve's son agreed that this was probably the true story,

so, i decided to roam around the fox river headwaters, fish, look around, and try to find out,

first dawn drove an aging bronco torturous miles of winding two-wheel ruts, eventually sliding a canoe down wet grasses to pond waters, scattering nesting sandhill cranes, disturbing a beaver family slapping their tails making a hasty retreat,

fast rising sun burning off cool morning mist, drying icy beads in spider webs,

black flies constantly hovered, biting clouds of hungry
mosquitoes, an endless swarm, around a pond dogleg,
portaging two ancient beaver dams, finally arriving at
flooded muskeg meadow of river meanderings, one
plump brookie already in creel,

large brown fish hawk lazily circling as the high noon
when i saw nick, shadowy figure resting under some
second growth pines in the distance, where the marsh
grasses turned to upland soils,

trace of bacon grease and streak of dried condensed
milk in his beard, apple butter pancake and onion
sandwich lunch set before him, laughing at me,

greenhorn trout fisherman furiously grasping at small
willow bushes, ass and billfold valuables soaked by
sudden icy plunge, finally pulling free of sinkhole ooze,
cold shock reminder of tragedy waiting the unwary alone
in the woods,

nick mocking the foolish who fish during hot noon
when high sky and bright sun make trout wary,

temptation to wave, holler adams down to chat, tell
fishing lies, smoke, but, quickly recalling he did not
like to fish "with other men,"

so i left him to the bitterns high up among the pine,
cedar, and birches, let him have his dreamy nap,
knowing later when dark purple clouds and orange
sky turn to dusk,

bottle of grasshoppers around his neck, flour sack

tied to his waist, he will climb over the log pile amid
cool evening shadows, this time working the "big
fish," plying sandy pebbles and gravel further, maybe

even into the swamp

before falling asleep that night, i thought about splake finding
the beginnings of the fox river, the big two-hearted, and like old
"papa hem" fishing for the exotic upper peninsula brook trout.
upon rising the next morning, i decided that i would postpone
paying respect to my grandfather and grandmother and instead visit
grand marais.

i left seney in the early morning darkness with a couple of
black coffees to go from the local restaurant heading the twenty-
five miles north on michigan highway 77 to grand marais. daylight
was breaking through the clouds. a bright sun was warming the
lake superior harbor. i drove down the steep hill that led into
grand marais. as i reached the bottom of the hill i noticed a sign
that read "the superior hotel" on an old wood-framed building. i
have always been drawn to an old-fashioned, simpler lifestyle. i
stopped in the hotel to ask about the possibility of getting a room
overnight. i met vivian stefani, who was serving coffee to a couple
of older gentlemen sitting on the high stools at the soda fountain.
vivian described the single versus double-bed accommodations and
prices, making clear that the "w.c." and bath were located at the
end of the hotel's hallway.

i ageed to take a double-bed room at the hotel's "boarding
house" and while drinking a much needed coffee i learned the
history of the hotel from vivian. the building was constructed in
1894. originally, it had been the private residence of john hunt, an
engineer with the manistique railway. about 18 years later joseph
laplant purchased the house and opened the "pippen hotel" there.
in 1939, alfred lungquist, vivian's father bought the business and
renamed it the superior hotel. the lundquists provided one of the
family blood lines for the community of grand marais. after the

decline of the lumber industry in grand marais, alfred had been a commercial fisherman on lake superior until his retirement. for at least a short while, vivian had been married to a grand marais swedish-italian gentlemen, a union that produced a son and daughter before orestes stefani disappeared.

vivian told me that bob at the sportsman's bar, kiddy-corner across the street from the superior hotel, should be able to recommend a local fisherman who might help me find the beginnings of the fox river. she also explained that two blocks east of the sportsman bar i could find the burt township school building and the school's library.

bob was a short, musclar looking guy. after we perused a topo-map of northern schoolcraft county, he suggested that a local young man, ward pratt, would make my best choice for a fishing guide. bob gave me ward's address and telephone number. i decided to try and connect with him later in the day.

on the street corner outside of the sportsman bar there was this huge barrel-like structure, which i would have to ask vivian about later during my stay in grand marais.

i was not surprised to discover that the burt township high school principal was also the school's librarian. miss penny barney told me that the school building had been built in 1929. the school opened with 9 teachers and 60 or so students. miss barney surmised it was probably the only k-through twelve-grade school system still operating in the state of michigan.

i was intrigued to discover that the burt township school library had a slim paperback collection of poems by the mysterious t. kilgore splake, titled *pictured rocks memories*. i gave penny a few dollars and we made a copy of the *pictured rocks memories* poems on a small canon personal copier that looked like it had already been used for many years.

i found ward pratt's apartment in an old tar-shingled house on alger street. i told him about the reason for my sudden odyssey and interest in finding the fox river, using the names of hemingway and splake very generously. we agreed on a trip to find the fox river's schoolcraft county beginnings the next morning. ward told me he would have fishing rods, nightcrawlers and bug dope and pick me up at 5 o'clock in front of the bayshore market on braziel street.

the day was reasonably warm so i decided i would to have my lunch and read the new poetry of splake on the lake superior breakwater. at the superior shore market, i bought a good-sized wedge of cheddar and a warm quart of blatz beer. hiking down canal street to the concrete breakwater stretching out into lake superior, i passed by the grand marais maritime museum, which for many years had been the united states coast guard station. close to the coast guard station was the light keeper's museum, which had been constructed and run by the coast guard administration until it was decommissioned from service.

separating the maritime and light keeper's museums were new grand marais condominiums on coast guard point. gazing at the condos i marveled at how nice wealth must be. those who could afford the condo-purchase price would have a front window that would be like a daily postcard exhibiting the different grand marais and upper peninsula seasons. a condominium resident could wake up each morning and feel a part of the year's spring, summer, autumn, and winter scenery.

i assumed that the truly rich would most likely not possess any appreciation for the marvelous changings of nature. the condo owners might feel better entertained watching the reruns of "the lawrence welk show," a favorite soap opera, or "the price is right" on their television set. for the older condo people their health could be very important. if someone in grand marais gets sick there are no doctors available and the nearest hospitals are munising memorial in munising, michigan, and helen newberry joy in newberry, michigan. for the very aged residents, grand marais did not have any senior citzen assisted apartments with professional care available.

nestled in a concrete corner on the lake superior breakwater i nibbled on the cheddar, sipped the warm blatz, and turned the pages of splake's poems in his *pictured rocks memories*. there were several broken-hearted poetic laments to young ladies who had failed to see splake's inner warmth and larger intelligence. the collection also had short poems describing sable falls and sand dunes, the log slide, au sable point lighthouse, and a very successful fishing expedition.

in particular i found a few poems that provided a surprisingly perceptive voice for the forgotten lost poet: "rx for a tired persona" and "alger county reminisences."

rx for a tired presence

a climate where the air is fresh and
surroundings quiet,

some rain some sunshine,

fewer people, more animals and birds,

forest leaves for the footsteps' carpet
and moonshadows for a roof,

traveling by foot, moving slowly,

worms, if the fish are biting.

alger county reminiscence

beyond the crabgrass and radar range,
past the tri-level with aluminum siding and
swimming pool is nature's unpackaged
reality,

the warmth of a sunny spring day with
fresh smelling forest scents,

a gentle breeze that toys with white puffs
of clouds against an azure backdrop,

and winding sparkling stream that plays
its mischievous may melody.

vivian kindly invited me to have dinner with her family at the stefani table in the parlor of the lake superior hotel. immediately after being introduced to her son and daughter, their wives and husbands and kids, i of course completely forgot their names.

vivian's venison stew was delicious, with lots of chili, oregano, peppers and garlic garlic garlic. her dessert, "italiano gelato," was a special way to finish my day.

someone at the table explained that the pickle barrel that i had seen earlier in the day was built in 1926 by the pioneer cooperage company of chicago for william donahey. donahey was the creator of the famous "teenie-weenie" comic strip that had been published by the *chicago tribune* newspaper. following the death of cartoonist donahey, the barrel has been an ice cream stand, information booth, gift shop, and now a museum for donahey's comic drawings.

knowing that tomorrow morning would come very early, i thanked vivian and her family for their company and the fine dinner feast, retiring upstairs to blow some serious and solid sweet zzzzzz's.

ward picked me up in front of the bayshore market about 5 the following morning. he was driving a vintage light green chevy pickup truck with a considerable amount of rust eating away at the body. i told ward, "sum-bitch, guy, you should get a can of black spray paint at the hardware store and quickly turn your pickup truck into a camouflaged land rover."

we left grand marais driving west on highway 58. ward explained there was another road to the kingston plains area south of grand marais that was called the "adams trail." he added that the grand marais and munising natives still use both m-27 and the adams trail as the name of the road we were traveling on this morning.

we drove past the parking lot area for the tourists who hike the sable waterfall path into lake superior. ward volunteered that this was just another waterfall site in the upper peninsula. he said every spring during "ice out" he would hike the falls trail. the raging sable river rapids pushing a torrent of winter debris was like god signaling that winter was over and it was time for a new beginning.

a few miles further along h-58 adams trail we passed sable lake and the start of the grand sable dunes. i had read that the dunes began years ago when the last northern glacier had retreated from this area. this movement left a deposit of gravels, sands and clay that made up the grand sable dunes. an interested hiker can trek across the "perched dunes" and stand at the edge and look down 300 feet to the lake superior waters. ward told me about the wild summer peas and the mysterious deer that leave footprints in the sand and apparently vanish at the sight of visitors. he also explained that at the far eastern heights of the grand sable dunes there was a "ghost forest" of ancient trees that carbon dating says are over 10,000 years old.

driving through an early morning lake superior fog, we passed the turn-off to the log slide and later the parking lot at the hurricane river and au sable lighthouse trail. as the morning's first dawn began streaking the eastern horizon, we passed the fire scarred pine stumps remaining on the kingston plains. ward told me that at the turn of the century during the height of the lumbering industry approximately 7,000 acres of white pine trees were cut in this area. he also said that after the decline of timbering, several forest fires had burned across the kingston plains, leaving the old stumps as history for the pictured rocks lake superior visitor.

as ward pulled his pickup truck off the adams trail onto a two-tire-track trail, i told him "you ought to have a four-wheel-drive truck, so that you would never get stuck." he replied, "that would be pretty expensive, so i just remember to drive carefully," adding, "if i get stuck, i can just get out, cut some small branches and make myself a corduroy bridge."

ward pulled over and parked at an unnamed pond that must have been fed by some underground spring, the beginning of the fox river waters. we paddled ward's thirteen foot grumman canoe to an old beaver dam and there made the first of three river portages until we finally came to a muskeg-marshy area where the river slowly meandered to a distant forest rise. after ward showed me how to cast a nightcrawler and let it float along the river's underground ledges, i got a bite and caught my first upper peninsula brook trout. of course i was extremely proud and thinking lo, behold, ernest hemingway and t. kilgore splake, ed michaels was now the complete angler. ward and i fished for another hour and some extra few minutes. following ward's habit or opinion, we returned the few other brook trout we caught to the fox river in order to grow larger for the next year.

ward explained his fishing philosophy with the new beaver dam that he discovered a few years ago in the middle of the pictured rocks lakeshore area. he told me the fishing was great and with every cast he caught a new good-sized rainbow trout. however, after the third visit to his trout honey-hole, he realized he had grown tired of taking dead fish back home. now his challenge was to find the trout and catch and release them. he no longer needed a trophy fish to show off to the people back in grand marais.

during our drive back to grand marais and my superior hotel lodging, ward told me his father had died of cancer when he was a small boy living in munising. while growing up with his mother in munising, he became close friends with his neighbor, roy eklund, a retired papermill employee who taught ward how to become a good fisherman. one of his best fishing experiences was the summer he camped with roy at the hurricane river and they lived off the whitefish, trout and menominee that they caught in lake superior.

ward also told me that after high school he had joined the navy and spent his first two years of duty at antarctica, and the rest of his enlistment term seeing the different people and places of the world. after his personal globetrotting to many different locations, he discovered he really liked the solitude and freedom of living in the upper peninsula wilderness. of course, he did not have a plastic blue-cross and blue-shield medical insurance card, but he had accepted that if one "lived" his life that meant taking risks. it seemed to me that he had a good life working at odd jobs around grand marais, doing carpentry work, painting houses, mowing lawns and shoveling out the winter blizzard snow.

with most of my day having vanished on our odyssey to find and fish the fox river waters, i wanted to get set and be ready to continue my traveling west early the next morning.

i stopped at the lake street office for *the great lakes pilot* newspaper and discussed with editor rick capogrossa putting a classified advertisement in the next issue of his publication. we agreed on the short statement that read:

wanted
information on t. kilgore splake
please contact
edward michaels
p.o. box 508
battle creek, michigan 49016
michaels@chartermi.net

i also stopped at the endress and sons fish market on morris street in grand marais and bought some smoked whitefish fillets to snack on while turning the tranny miles toward iron mountain the next day. thanks to vivian's generosity, i stored my picnic treat in her parlor refrigerator until i left in the morning.

awake and off early driving down h-58, traveling over the same miles that ward and i had the day before, i decided to turn off the highway and see the log slide. the pictured rocks national lakeshore service had constructed a sturdy wooden platform overlooking the sandy log slide that also provided an excellent view of the grand sable dunes in the east. earlier i had discovered the log slide was an important place during the lumbering boom in the grand marais area, and narrow-gauge railroads would haul the cut timbers to the log slide. there they would cut the logs loose to slide down the 500 feet high sand dune where they were floated along the lake superior shore into the grand marais sawyers. i remember one of bob's sportsman bar tall-stool beer drinkers saying that often the logs would be smoking from the friction of rubbing together by the time they reached the lake below.

a little later, but still early morning, my car was the only one in the hurricane river au sable lighthouse trail parking lot. the lighthouse path is an easy mile-and-a-half walk into a clearing where you find the red brick lightkeeper's house, the white cylinders of the lighthouse tower, and another dwelling that was for the lighthouse service employees. the au sable lighthouse ownership had been transferred to the national park service in 1968. after that the national park service restored the lighthouse to its 1910 condition. as i hiked back to the parking lot, i chose to walk along the lake superior shore, where i saw the remains of three lake freighters that had foundered in earlier lake superior storms. according to a park service "diorama" they were probably the *sitka*, which sank on october 4, 1904, the *gale staples*, which went down on october 1, 1918, and the *mary jarecki*, that ran on a reef in july 4, 1883.

while recrossing the kingston plains area with its burned-stump sentinels of past history, i suddenly got the ispheming wjpd 92.3 "big country" fm radio station coming in loud and clear on my car radio. the morning's "early driving" country and western music program was hosted by brian morrisey at the ispheming wjpd f.m. station. suddenly i was lost in the words of patsy cline singing "crazy" and "i fall to pieces." morrisey also had a radio highlight moment for the "two hanks," williams and snow, playing their recordings "i'm so lonesome i could cry," and "i'm movin' on." i felt closer to the harsh reality of getting by in life when brian closed out his "early driving" show with eddy arnold's "make the world go away," and the classic country and western ballad by kitty wells, "it wasn't god who made honky-tonk angels."

those "hurtin' heart" songs brought back the sadness of my recent romantic breakup with a young battle creek girl and kellogg community college graduate. paula middleton suddenly decided that she had finally had enough of the punishing michigan winters with the snow and arctic temperatures. she moved to finish her college degree program in warmer, sunnier southern california. beyond my aching woe, at least i had a tattoo that said "i love paula" in polish inside a red rose on my arm as a reminder of our serious past love.

while turning the dusty adams trail miles to munising, i also thought about the basic honesty that country and western song lyrics possessed. they seemed like a musical poetry that cut deeply into the hearts of the human experiences that people have in their lives. i wondered what the basic upper peninsula bard, t. kilgore splake might have to say about that opinion.

suddenly I was driving past the melstrand city limits sign. i quickly slowed down stopping near the gas pumps at the melstrand store in order to check things out. the store owner skip was working this morning. i bought a can of diet-coke and asked him if my seney friend, bruce clark, had been in his store. skip replied that he sees bruce every three or four days when he hitch-hikes in from his ross lake camp to check the general delivery mail. skip also volunteered an additional footnote to bruce, saying recently he had received a letter with serious perfume scents on it that was addressed to the "maelstrom store."

as i slowed to pass through the three-cornered stop sign intersection that was van meer, i noticed the bear trap inn off to my left. there were already a couple of cars in the parking lot so i guessed two or three of the locals were having an early morning beer and chaser start. the descent into the city of munising gave me a beautiful sight of the blue munising bay waters and what i learned later was "grand island" in the bay. i could see small chunks of ice or tiny ice bergs that were still floating in the munising bay. i thought what the hell, it was still early may, and the cold snowy elements of winter had not yet completely vanished. i parked in front of the navigator restaurant on munising's main street and chose a window table looking out on munising bay while i checked out the breakfast menu. it was still before the memorial day holiday and the start of three months of tourist season in munising and across the upper peninsula, so the navigator restaurant was almost empty of other morning breakfast customers.

an old man wearing a navy-looking hat walked up to me and said, "good morning, you are too early for the first pictured rocks boat trip." that is how i met everett morrison, a retired lake pictured rocks cruise captain. his grandson, peter, was now a captain of the "miss superior" and was going to take his boat out later that morning and do a "shake down" trip. everett said the first boat tour of the season would begin on may 29th and that i ought to think seriously about coming back to munising to see the old wooden lighthouse on grand island, miner's castle and chapel beach up close on a boat trip.

i told everett that i had driven in to munising from grand marais this morning on the old adams trail, passing the bear trap inn in van meer. everett paused, chuckled, and replied, "yes, it used to be the old club majestic, run by the maciejewski family back in the old lumbering days". he explained how the old man maciejewski who ran the tavern and whore house ran away to detroit with one of the club's working girls. he said the two maciejewski daughters, fernedez and genevieve, took over running the tavern and that even the locals thought the two girls were lesbians. until their recent deaths it used to seem like great fun to drive out and have a beer or three at the club majestic, teasing the "silly sisters." my morning breakfast friend everett paused and sighed then and said, "ah, but our history is always changing, eh?"

after breakfast i decided to look over the impressive inventory at the falling rock bookstore across main street from the navigator.

i met one of the bookstore owners, jeff dwyer, who told me
his wife, nancy, was upstairs taking care of some of the store's
bookkeeping business. jeff told me that nancy and he had bought
the store about six years ago and acquired an inventory of over
30,000 new and used book titles in their store.

when i asked jeff about my mystery upper peninsula poet,
t. kilgore splake, he replied that the name didn't sound familiar.
but after thinking for a moment he told me a splake is an upper
peninsula planter trout. then he told me that author kurt vonnegut
had a character called kilgore trout in many of his books. after
taking a few minutes to check his book files for more information,
jeff discovered that vonnegut's *breakfast of champions* and *god
bless you, mr. rosewater* were vonnegut books with the trout
character.

we found a used copy of *breakfast of champions* on the falling
rock bookstore's special 99 cents sales table, which i purchased to
add to my other readings about harry haller in hesse's *steppenwolf*
pages. while jeff was making change and wrapping my paperback
book, nancy came downstairs and jeff introduced us, telling her
about my t. kilgore splake search and adventure. nancy told me
when they first arrived in munising, erika french, the proprietor of
the corktown bar, had been dating an older bearded man who many
said called himself a poet. nancy added that erika's daughter, tara,
was still working at the corktown bar and was probably there this
morning.

i thanked the dwyers for their information. i took my copy
of *breakfast of champions*, and walked down the block to the
corktown bar where i found tara french working the bar. after
telling her about my search for a poet named splake, she replied
that her mother and he were very close friends not too long ago.
she added that after her mother died of breast cancer six years ago,
splake moved away from munising. tara told me she thought she
had saved a writing or two that splake had shared with her mother
and left behind. she added i should give her a chance to check on
it and if she found anything i was very welcome to make copies of

the pages. it was necessary for me to stay overnight in munising. as luck or fortune might have it, another old upper peninsula hotel existed in munising. i checked into the bay house for a single-bed room for overnight.

while waiting for the finish of tara's investigation i stopped at the munising office of *porcupine press publication*. after a short conversation with the editor, michael van den branden, i paid for a "help me find splake" classified advertisement. i also hiked into munising falls, a fantastic 50 foot ribbon of water dropping into munising creek and floating eventually into lake superior. a brief visit was paid to the alger county heritage center on washington street in munising, where i looked over the collections of the area's past history. at sand point beach i sat at a picnic table and quickly turned the first twenty pages of vonnegut's *breakfast of champions*. i had a spectacular view of the old wooden lighthouse on grand island, directly across from munising bay and my sand point respite.

later that afternoon tara presented me with her discovery of a long splake poem titled "christmas cards" she had found in her mother's personal belongings. we went to the munising news newspaper office and made copies of the pages. i also purchased a file-folder in which i hoped to store the splake writings. then, in a rare moment of exposing my male madness, i asked tara, "if you do not have a serious boy or girl friend in munising, i would like to take you to dinner later this evening."

i was extremely pleased when tara replied that she would be glad to have dinner with me. i picked her up at her home on the corner of walnut and superior streets and discovered she lived in a nice older "little house" on the west end. from the back window of her house one could to see munising bay and grand island. despite rather hokey little abner type advertisements for "scurmshus vittles" where a diner could get "lishis country fixin'" we chose the dogpatch restaurant for our dining. after carefully perusing the fancy menu we agreed to have the new york steak dinner for two. returning from the salad bar i told tara "i could have easily made a real meal just eating there."

while finishing up the german torte dessert, tara told me how hard it had been growing up in a small town without a dad. after her father had married erika he lost his job at the kimberly-clark paper mill in munising and spent his days drinking and drawing welfare checks. tara said when he finally disappeared one day, her mother never tried to find him for child-support payments, figuring her life was better with him simply gone.

tara agreed to my suggestion that we do a quick "pub-crawl" of the munising bars before finishing our date. we had beers at the country connection and sydney's where i told tara this was my first visit to the upper peninsula and i really liked all that i had seen so far. i explained that i had been going to college or working factory jobs to earn more college tuition money to go back to school, and now i was trying to establish my position at the kellogg company in battle creek. we avoided the corktown bar, tara's place of employment. after draft beers at the barge inn and shooters we ended up at the trails end bar on superior street.

while sipping a lowenbrau, tara explained that her life as a young single girl in munising was very lonely. she believed the most important part of a successful relationship was the ability of a man and woman to talk about interesting things. she read books and magazines, rented creative netflix movies and checked over the internet locations for things happening on the american artistic scene. it did not surprise me when she said that all of the guys she had graduated from high school with never had any new ideas other than hunting, weekend television sports, drinking, and sex with girls. with our evening almost finished, tara told me how she was saving money in order to start classes at northern michigan university in marquette. she was determined to see if she could paint and how far she might be able to go with her talent.

tara gave me her munising mailing address and was looking forward to handwritten personal letters from me rather than less intimate computer e-mail messages. after giving her a kiss on her cheek and telling her i had a great time she said, "ted, come back to munising some weekend, and we can shuck and jive with whatever band is playing at the knotty club okay?"

with iron mountain on my immediate mind i left the bay house warm bed early in order to make some quiet tranny miles west. suddenly i discovered i was in the small village of christmas and like holiday trimmings everything was painted red. the objibawa casino, knotty club and foggy's restaurant were all decorated to resemble a christmas celebration. i made a fast stop to check out santa's workshop on st. nicolas avenue but it was not open yet. there was simply tourist trap stuff for the spring and summer travelers to buy. there was also a sign on the front door that said "deposit your christmas cards for the christmas postmark in this box, sandra." behind the santa's workshop building there was a small zoo of animals. in one cage there was a black bear continuously pacing the four corners of his prison. i thought holy waugh and then some, there is something worse than death, wishing i had the courage to set the black bear free, to survive or die in the upper peninsula wilderness.

arriving in marquette i drove down third street, looking for a place to get coffee and maybe breakfast. i noticed a man opening the snowbound book store so i stopped and met mr. snowbound, the bookstore proprietor, ray nurmi. after asking him about kurt vonnegut and t. kilgore splake, ray replied that he knew about the vonnegut character kilgore trout but didn't have the book *god bless you, mr. rosewater* in his bookstore's inventory at the moment. he told me he had heard about the writings of t. kilgore splake but had never had a chance to read any of his works. at ray's recommendation i continued my drive up third street and had my breakfast at the sweetwater café, a health-food restaurant with mostly vegetarian selections on their menu. i was more than satisfied with my garlic bagel and english black tea which definitely quieted my tummy dwarf. after my breakfast pause i found the peter white library and did a quick search for information on kilgore. i learned that kilgore trout was a fictionalized version of kurt vonnegut's close writing friend theodore sturgeon. i also learned about a literary opinion that kilgore trout was simply the alter ego of kurt vonnegut.

kilgore trout made his major literary appearances in vonnegut's *breakfast of champions* and *god bless you, mr. rosewater* but also appeared in *timequake, jailbird,* and *galapagos* publications. trout's only known residences were hyannis, massachuetts, and ilium and cohoes, new york. i discovered that he had written 117 books and over 2000 short stories, been married three times and divorced three times with one child leo, a veteran of the vietnam war. because of his reclusivity his science-fiction books and stories had not been accepted by the normal american book publishers. trout's major publisher was the world classics library, a firm that specialized in producing pornographic novels and magazines. this meant his books and stories possessed lurid covers and were used as filler in girlie magazines. a biography article said that when trout was not writing books and stories he worked as an installer of aluminum combination storm windows and screens. a novel *venus on the half-shell* was attributed to trout but it was actually written by phillip jose farmer.

with my marquette hours disappearing like precious rat bastard time, i still wanted to see the city's ore loading docks before continuing my drive to iron mountain. i took presque isle avenue to north lake shore boulevard and drove north to the ore docks. i pulled into the parking lot as the lake freighter roger blough was taking on a cargo of iron ore pellets from the cleveland-cliffs negaunee and ispheming open-pit mines. checking over the road map, i saw i was not too far from the iron mountain destination. i left marquette on highway m-41, passing through negaunee and ispheming then taking a hard left south i aimed my artful dodger auto-tranny down m-96 toward the iron mountain city limits.

my mind was lost in a momentary blur of afternoon yooper fog. suddenly the minnesota public radio station had a classical music program "objects in the mirror" directed by julia schrenkler coming in loud and clear. she told the listening audience she was playing the schubert "trout dancing sonata" this afternoon, hoping it would bring luck to the yooper anglers fishing for trophy rainbows and brookies.

watching the miles click past on my odometer i thought of my grandfather luigi meneguzzo. he moved to iron mountain in 1906 to work in the iron mines. after reading luigi's letters and his wife's diary entries i felt i had a good idea of what life was like back then and what the conditions of growing up in the little italy section of iron mountain were. luigi would write frequent letters to his wife while she was still living in castlegomberto, telling her that when he was on the family farm back home he worked like a slave and still wasn't able to save any money. he was earning good money in the mine and sending dollars back to italy, so carissima could come live with him in iron mountain. he told carissima that he loved and missed her badly. they would live in iron mountain for eight or ten years and then decide about staying in america or returning home to live in italy. luigi got his wife's immigration papers in order, told her what steamships to come to america on, and reminded her to make sure that the address on the trunk was correct in order to pass successfully through the immigration inspection in new york.

when carissima and his daughter theresa finally arrived in iron mountain in may, 1909, the meneguzzos rented a house from the oliver mining company. iron mountain's little italy was on the north side of town, near luigi's job at the chapin mine. ten months after his wife arrived in the new country a son was born to the meneguzzos and they named him luigi ii. for six days a week luigi worked ten hours a day mining iron ore at the chapin mine shafts. it was the burden of carissima to manage the home and take care of raising theresa and young luigi junior. she would wash her husband's mining clothes that were permeated with iron ore stains by scrubbing them in strong soap then hanging them outside to dry. they raised vegetables and herbs in a small garden beside their home and made their own wine in basement barrels.

many other italian families raised chickens as well as owned a horse and a cow. the people with a cow could get milk and make butter which they often sold to other families in the italian neighborhood. the wives continued to cook as they had in the old country, with polenta (corn meal mush) bayna cauda (warm gravy), and gnocchi (potato dumplings) their favorite meal choices. most of the italian families made their own tomato paste from ripe tomatoes that were cooked and strained through cheesecloth. the residents in little italy used many home remedies to handle their illnesses. balsam pitch was applied to draw out infections, plantain leaves helped heal sores, and warm olive oil was used for muscle aches.

on sundays and holidays the new italian citizens would make sure to have a good time. often the men would hold drilling contests to see which of the miners could drill the farthest in a period of time. others played bocce, a bowling game that needed a court of flat earth. the italians had a great love of music and during their celebrations the older women would sit and crochet while the young boys and girls would dance to music that bands would play. some men would spend their sundays and holidays rushing the can, drinking in one of the frequent iron mountain saloons. there were frequent tavern fights between the miners and lumberjacks who held no love in common and italians who started fighting over which part of italy was the best. for the young children in iron mountain, store bought toys were almost unheard of but the kids thrived on occasional candy store treats. a piece of ice to nibble on from the ice wagon was also special. on christmas morning all the iron mountain children were joyed to find a stocking filled with an orange, chocolate bar, an apple, nuts and candies.

while driving from marquette to iron mountain i had to ask myself, why did my grandfather choose to leave the farm and his family in italy and emigrate to an unknown future in america? 1906 was well before the world had shrunk with jet flights and the immediate use of computer communications. back then, if you did not like the new country, tough luck, you were there. with three other brothers, luigi's inherited share of the family farm would have been small, and probably only a continuance of his poverty.

i think the major reason for luigi's decision to come to america was to escape. he would likely be leaving a rigid-minded father as well as getting away from a small village priest applying narrow religious beliefs. he would also be free of the family relations and their conservative opinions they took to their cemetery graves. i believe luigi saw the prospect of a successful new life in a fresh young country.

from the wide variety of lodging accommodations on stephenson avenue in iron mountain. i chose to get a room at the motel six. at the motel counter i bought a modest paperback book *born iron: a history of iron mountain michigan*, by edward ansel mccloud. a quick check revealed the book had been published by miskwabik press in calumet, michigan, by editor ed gray. i also selected some of the tourist brochures from the motel's turnstile rack, pamphlets on iron mining, the menominee range historical museum, and the history of the cornish pumping engine for later reading. then i drove over to fredricks floral store on carpenter avenue and ordered a modest cemetery piece i told the lady i would pick up tomorrow morning. feeling completely exhausted, i decided to have a take-out-pizza and six pack of blue ribbon for my dinner at the motel six room.   while nibbling on small pieces of pepperoni and small salty anchovies i read the pages of splake's "christmas cards" i made from tara's copy.

christmas cards

(erika-erika-erika)

signed sealed postage attached
"moma" holiday cards
waiting calumet mailsack
"peace dove"
"bobblehead snowmen"
along with personal photos
cliffs poet tree with

tibetan prayer flag
poems postcards pictures
splake at the lectern
evening poetry reading
calumet art center
rear closeup shot
showing ponytail and bald spot
bard 'res' writing corner
working space organizer
calendar legal tablets folders
chai green tea bags
new book volumes
paul auster's *invisible*
phillip roth's *humbling*
new writing notes
manuscript pages waiting
hoping munising address
reaches young tara
corktown barmaid erika's daughter
wondering if her mother
shared our relationship
after last call tavern hours
discussing my day's writing
another envelope seeking grady
son of old friend pat oneill
ironwood post office box
last location
curious if grady had heard
about our wild young times
one sunday morning
rolling over an old chevy
saint augustine church front steps
western michigan students
classes on kalamazoo campus
learning literary correctness

writing rules and regulations
dull college professors
discouraging creative experiments
beauty measured
only from past works
pat off to marines
san diego boot camp
desert military maneuvers
running across barren wastelands
yelling "recon recon recon"
while i worked paper mill hours
kalamazoo vegetable parchment company
11 p.m. to 7 a.m. trick
earning necessary dollars
raising daughter robin lynn
sad teenage marriage
doomed to quickly fail
pat's wife valerie
saving him from nursing home hell
prison captivity without
marsh wheelings
rum soaked crooks
cigar smoke haze
cueball clicking off eight
riding green rail felt
end pocket call
pool game victory
icy pitcher of beer
suds always on tap
someone declaring
"jacks or better to open
whores and fours wild
read-em and weep"
rock and roll rhythms
country and blues do-wahs

fats domino joe turner bill haley
"chantilly lace"
"shake rattle and roll"
"rock around the clock"
instead with vacant demented others
lysol-ammonia stink
coloring with crayons
arts and crafts afternoon time
like old elementary school days
ghosts of dick jane spot watching
bing and andrews sisters singing
rare sinatra ballad
finnish jug band
for special holiday treat
graybeard with .357 fevers
other writers
their black empty depressions
falling to high caliber attraction
hemingway brautigan d.a. levy
hunter thompson saying
"football season is over
this won't hurt"
lew welch
disappearing with hunting rifle
desert wilderness trek
body never found
david foster wallace
leaving his "infinite jest"
but splake still has
poems to write
songs to sing
no time to die now
like 92-year old
activist alice mcgrath
"oh to be 70 again"

needing 89th birthday party
like john demjanjuk
ww-ii holocaust suspect
aging poet
not wishing to be young again
or returning to smith family home
that was never happy
with time running out
recalling my life spent running
escaping narrow boundaries
rigid three rivers demands
mother margaret father emery
their parental "this way" rules
in family with serious expectations
always demanding excellence
endless piano lessons
practicing scales and etudes
jock sport games waiting
madly chasing after
american bitch goddess success
leaving girls to love
missing other friends
driven by quiet fears
taking serious risks
pushing always pushing
beyond normal limits
humdrum sameness of others' lives
seeking leading role
no second rate actor lines
like virginia woolf
a room of one's own
needing a place to write
silent anchorite cell
solitude to reinvent myself
hear sounds inside my head

learn to live
with darkness inside my loneliness
no more greenwich village
walkup apartment sublet
macdougal street
piano bars and clubs
now sad façade
place for wannabes
ambitious people without talent
those talking their art
also lost
cheap north beach "beat pads"
jazz poetry marijuana
in dark night fog
buoy horns moaning
no more "six gallery" readings
cheap chianti melodies
vesuvio's bar
long gone memories
san francisco's
city lights bookstore
making ferlinghetti dollars
no new creative art
shaking human consciousness
today's poet needing
cheap bardic 'res'
lamp clawfoot tub hotplate sauce pan
warm hudson bay blanket
with samuel beckett wisdom
try fail try again fail better
while others
never asking
"is this all there is"
lacking drive
cunts or cojones

to make something great
mediocre beings on sidelines
enjoying buying adult toys
talking about the weather
safe default gossip item
while constantly changing tv channels
remote their only power
poet living alone
no more smiths
family or close relatives
few other artistic friends
like quiet shadowy
man without a country
seeking sacred location
while his words become music
dancing in the brain-skull cavity
finally finding "home"
harsh keweenaw peninsula beauty
growing close to wisdom
sitting atop of
million-year-old basaltic cliffs
high rocky escarpment summit
like tutankhamen's tomb
golden ships ready to sail
on journey to another world
as graying poet's soul
resembles the ancient tree
in michael loukinen's film
"the old man in the woods"
waiting coming storm
fierce winds blowing
arctic season of long white
creative obituary already written
with interesting tales of tom
no one will read

or care about
but hoping for a few minutes
someone somewhere whispers
"he wrote poetry with his camera"

    after reading the pages from splake's "christmas cards" poem,
i thought about his reference to the calumet art center. sometime
in his life he made the move from munising to calumet to live and
write. there was also a specific statement in "christmas cards" to
the "basaltic cliffs" as well as an identification of a cliffs poet tree.
this sounds like splake possessed his own special place to retire
to when he needed the quiet opportunity to be alone and think.
the writings also referred to his college education, sad teenage
marriage failure, the pain of losing a much younger girlfriend,
and the hatred of what he called "nursing home hell." the voice
of splake definitely sounds like a driven artist, mentioning the
challenge of the bitch goddess of success, black .357 fevers, and
using the quote of samuel beckett, "try, fail, try again, fail better"
to fuel his creative focus and energy.   most certainly "christmas
cards" serves as splake's future creative obituary, yet it declares
he still had poems to write, in order to move beyond the humdrum
mediocrity of other artists. it was also interesting that splake
wished to be remembered briefly for making poetry with his
camera.
    the next morning i drank my coffee at a small café called
"the coffee corner" on south stephenson avenue. having a few
extra minutes to waste before fredrick's florist shop opened, i
turned some early pages in the kurt vonnegut book *breakfast
of champions*. i was quickly attracted to the dramatic tension
between vonnegut's major characters, a car dealer salesman,
dwayne hoover, and the writer, kilgore trout. after putting
breakfast of champions away, i thought of my old college
professor, paul bach, who told us in his class one day that he read
the play *waiting for godot* every two or three years and always

found something new in that experience. i wondered if vonnegut's *breakfast of champions* might also reveal new ideas through future rereadings.

today's business was to put a memorial wreath at the gravesite of luigi and carimissa meneguzzo. i also wanted to find out what history still remained of the iron mining industry in iron mountain.

it was easy to find the iron mountain cemetery park. i also had no trouble finding the substantial gray marble headstone that said "luigi meneguzzo 1880 to 1936 and carissima meneguzzo 1885 to 1947." i was pleased to see they did not have some special religious inscription on the gravestone. i assumed that their funerals were long and drawn out affairs. the italians always wanted to make sure the surviving spouse was properly grief stricken, and, also to prevent any possible witches leaving the "evil eye" to curse the rest of the family.

carissima's iron mountain diary told about her husband's job at the chapin mine. there was an elevator-cage that would lower him to the level where he was mining. before the invention of the air-drill, two men would work together, with one man holding the mining drill and the other hitting it with a sledge hammer. the chapin mine was called the biggest and the wettest of the iron mines. luigi and the other miners wore rubber suits and boots to work in. carissima's writings told about many things that were related to luigi's mining activities. she mentioned "hanging walls," "lagging," "pillars," "faults," "drifts," "cribbing," "capping," and the "mining skips."

the families were always worried about getting a serious contagious disease like tuberculosis or typhoid. after a mining shift luigi would shower and change his clothes in the dry house. dry closets were used to hoist the miner's excreta to the surface where it was dumped. the dry closets were regularly washed out and thoroughly soaked with lime. each month luigi and the other miners had a dollar deducted from their earnings that went to pay for their medical services.

edward ansel mccloud in his book *born from iron* stated that the chapin mine was the giant of the menominee range mining operation and its first shipment of iron ore was in 1880. mccloud said that in 1901, the oliver mining company, a subsidiary of the u.s. steel corporation, aquired the chapin mining property. chapin mining had record years of producing ore and profits for the oliver company and was called "payroll of the north." in order to drain the mines and keep them free of water the oliver company created a powerful pumping machine that was called the cornish pump, in honor of the iron miners in england.

mccloud notes that fatal mining accidents were not uncommon in chapin mining operations. miners were killed frequently by falling ore or timbers, mine explosions while setting a charge, getting caught by tram cars that had broken loose, and falling into the open mine pit. as explained in *born from iron* a depressed ore market in 1921 to 1922 shut down the chapin mine for eight months. during the great depression the chapin mine closed permanently on august 1, 1932. the conclusion of mccloud's mining history research said that rich iron ore still remained in the chapin mine but the cost of mining the depths made the product unmarketable.

i drove around the northside of iron mountain. with the changes that come from the history of passing years, i could find no evidence of where luigi went to work for several years of his life. for a few minutes i walked through displays of mining history at the menominee range historical museum. there were many pictures of iron mountain and the past years of mining, as well as a display of old work clothes stained with the red ore dust to remind the viewer of the past. there was a larger collection of mining artifacts at the iron mining museum, on kent street in iron mountain. i saw ore cars, jack hammers, drilling equipment, tuggers, scrapers, skips, and the old cornish mine engine that still rests inside the iron museum historical building. the museum brochure said the cornish pumping engine was 40 feet in diameter, weighed 160 tons, stood 54 feet above the mining building's floor and had a 40 foot flywheel. even by today's modern standards

i found the chapin mine's cornish pump a most impressive
technological phenomenon. it was also interesting to read the
names of the past chapin miners listed on a working roster hanging
from a museum wall. there was a fine collection of good paisanos:
corsi, fontecchio, petiori, fiorani, spigarelli, palloconi, bodini, and
corolla. like some kind of magic i found luigi meneguzzo's name
in one of the working miner's columns.

feeling certain that i would quickly use up the day's hours
with my cemetery visit and research of the iron mountain mining
history, i took my motel six room for another evening. i would
finish the vonnegut pages of breakfast of champions and be on the
road driving north the following morning. i had decided to find out
what i could about t. kilgore splake in the keweenaw peninsula and
village of calumet.

whether you are up early studying for the big grad school exam
or taking a dark morning piss in the kitchen sink after a night of
wild-ass boozing, it is called the brain-skull madness of the early
morning existentials. watching the iron mountain city limits fading
in my rearview mirror, i didn't have the minnesota public radio
station playing carl orff's "carmina burana," or ottorino respighi's
"the pines of rome." no deejay joking about the two kinds of
music in the world, country and western. absent too was the ghost
of the hossman, from wlac in gallatin, tenneseee, trying to sell me
royal crown hair dressing in between rock and roll songs. there
were many deer licking on the winter road salt and feeding on
fresh rye grass along the highway edge. i slowed down while my
mind focused on the characters and drama in vonnegut's *breakfast
of champions*.

the book concerns the famous hack writer kilgore trout,
hitchhiking to midland city to speak to a festival of arts convention.
he meets dwayne hoover who owns a pontiac car dealership and
believes after reading a trout short story that he is the only real
human being on the earth possessing free will. according to the
trout short story all human beings are robots who must be trained
to become agreeing machines rather than thinking machines.

according to *breakfast of champions* the american population has
no use for the arts, only sex, money, real estate, football games,
television, and alcohol.

trout believed that citizens should spend their time searching
for truth and beauty, loving a person for their body and soul
while laughing, dancing, and singing more. using the motto of
the general electric company, "progress is our most important
product," trout said the average american only wanted to "talk"
about fairness, brotherhood and happiness without doing anything
to achieve these things. i found the conclusion to *breakfast of
champions* very interesting as the character kilgore trout is begging
the author kurt vonnegut to please "make me young again, make
me young."

by the time i pulled into the village of calumet and drove down
fifth street the early dawn was making shadows. i later learned
it was saint anne's church that darkened the conglomerate café
doorway entrance. walking into the café i saw i was the only
customer. how nice, i thought i have always wanted to have
my own restaurant. i met geoff, the conglomerate café owner,
who brought me a cup of dark ethiopian coffee and pointed to
the breakfast menu written in chalk on a blackboard hung on the
wall. geoff told me that his wife, leah was in the back getting the
morning loaves of bread out of the oven and wrapping them for
today's customers. a few minutes later leah came into the café
wearing an apron that covered a baby boy or girl due sometime
before the first autumn frost.

i sighed when i discovered that the conglomerate café had
an internet connection. i was supposed to be on a vacation but i
wondered if i had received any new e-mail messages since leaving
battle creek. after booting up my laptop and checking, i was
surprised to find new messages from marquette and munising,
michigan. the first e-mail had the address of the northern
michigan university fine arts department and said:

ted ted teddy,

41

i noticed your advertisement in the lastest issue of the marquette monthly magazine and your request for information about t. kilgore splake. for a while splake and i were a couple, and we were also planning on getting married. so i fucked him, and gave him a blowjob now and then when i was having a period. i also saved the rough drafts of his book manuscripts as an insurance against some literary disaster destroying them. splake had a writing friend, richard yates, who used to put his unfinished manuscripts in the refrigerator freezer in case his apartment would burn down. anyhow, i have attached the chapbook manuscript for splake's "beyond ashes – a becoming." ted, please also note, i want to be treated anonymously, and i want no further connection with splake. if he is alive, i wish him only hard times, and if splake is dead, it would be nice to piss some cheap whiskey on his cemetery tombstone or where his ashes were scattered.

for your reading, if not enjoyment, "beyond ashes, ..."

kay lee's mother

while these words were ricocheting between my ears with a dull roar i checked out my second new e-mail message, from ryan kolbus in munising, michigan. ryan's letter said:

dear mr. michaels,

i read your advertisement about wanting information on t. kilgore splake in the recent copy of the porcupine press classified pages. splake and my father, j.b., were very close friends, as dad served as the executor for administering splake's estate when he died. i can remember him telling me about standing at a place called the "poet tree" in the

cliffs north of calumet, while another poet from wisconsin
turned over his burial urn and scattered the ashes below
the cliffs. splake also used to send my old man writings
that related to new book manuscripts to read and to give his
opinions on. however, i think that what he really wanted
was for someone else to have copies of his writings to save
for him, just in case something happened. after wrestling
through the papers that my dad left me when he died three
years ago, i have found the book draft for splake's "cliffs
notes." it is attached to this e-mail message, and if you
have any futher questions, please do not hesitate contacting
me.

yours truly

ryan kolbus

quickly i asked geoff and leah where in the small village of
calumet i might make printed copies of these two new e-mails.
geoff suggested i try the local library at the high school. leah said
i might have to check at michigan technological university's data
processing department in houghton.
    i discovered that sometimes people are just lucky. calumet's
assistant librarian, patty hall, connected my laptop to one of the
library's printers, and voila, there is a god, pages of the manuscript
came flowing into the printing machine's tray. i paid patty for the
service and added a few extra dollars for the library's morning
coffee and rolls fund.
    i left the library, and rented a street level single bedroom room
at the elms motel on the corner of elms and sixth street. i still
had most of the day in front of me so i decided to drive to copper
harbor at the far north end of the keweenaw peninsula, to see what
i could see.
    north of calumet i followed the lake superior shoreline
highway north to copper harbor. about one mile before passing

through eagle river i put the artful dodger in reverse and backed
to the entrance of the evergreen cemetery. wandering around
the cemetery and reading the inscriptions on the grave markers,
i found most of the headstones were for people who had lived in
the nearby clifton village or cliffs mine location. some were small
children who died during the severe influenza and yellow fever
epidemics. other grave sites were miners killed in accidents at the
cliffs mine.

one monument had the following inscription:

erected
to the memory of
rev. john bramwell
first rector of grave
church clifton lake
superior
who died at cliff mine
february 1st 1859
aged 37 years

back of the road i slowed down for the dogleg curve at jacob
falls. i saw the small white building with the sign "jam pot"
on it and pulled into the parking lot. i discovered the jam pot
was operated by the society of saint john, a monastery affiliated
with the ukrainian catholic church. the monks sell fruit cakes
and thimbleberry preserves to finance their life of monastic
contemplation. i was told that during the long keweenaw winters
they used their solitude to come closer to god through personal and
liturgical prayers.

listening to the monk's description of their monastic retreat, i
remembered reading the *seventh story mountain* and a selection of
poems by thomas merton in one of my college humanities classes.
merton was a trappist monk at the abbey of gethsemani in kentucky
and pursued a life of work, prayer, and religious contemplation.
while i did not support the order of the cistercian religious tenets,

i greatly admired merton for his serious meditations during his solitary retreats. on my way out of the jam pot i noticed the price on a fruit cake was $40.00. pulling out of the parking lot i saw a large new pole barn in the distance. also across the road from the jam pot was a holy transfiguration skete with a golden dome for sunday masses. pretty fancy buildings as well as an expensive outlay for a religious mission that embraces evangelical poverty.

on the bay in the small village of eagle harbor is the magnificent eagle river lighthouse with an octagonal brick lighthouse tower that was built in 1871. the eagle harbor light was necessary to protect the lake ships from the dangerous sawtooth reef in the nearby lake superior shallows. today the lighthouse is a nautical museum run by the keweenaw historial society of eagle harbor. i chose not to visit the museum as in robert frost's poem, if i lacked promises to keep, i still had miles to go before bedtime.

a few more miles up m-26 i turned onto the brockway mountain drive and slowly eased my tranny to the summit. the mountain had been named after dan brockway, an early pioneer who helped settle the town of copper harbor. brockway drive was the highest highway above sea level between the rocky and allegheny mountains. looking over the scenery i enjoyed a vast panorama of the keweenaw peninsula: lake bailey, the keweenaw mountain lodge and golf course, lake superior and a new a-frame cabin sticking out in the middle of my view. i thought of the old american cliché, this is the land of the brave and home of the free. if a person owns an acre or two on brockway mountain and wants a cottage, there it is in front of everyone else seeking to enjoy the untouched beauty of the summit.

in copper harbor i paid the admission and had a grand time walking through the historically restored fort wilkins property. it was an excellent example of a wise expenditure of tax dollars to save a valuable place in michigan's past history. stopping for a diet coke at a convenience store in copper harbor, i said hello to three backpackers who had their sleeping bags and backpack frames ready for the arrival of the "isle royale voyager iv" to take them across lake superior to a campsite on isle royale. surveying the eager hikers, their adventure looked like fun. maybe one spring soon it would be me trekking on the isle royale trails.

back on the road i drove down the lac la belle road, returning to calumet along the eastern lake superior shoreline. suddenly i was passing an ugly large chalet and several condo-apartments of the mount bohemia ski resort. for sake of earning dollars the t-bar system now ran from the bottom to the top of mount bohemia destroying the keweenaw wilderness scenery.

i came to an intersection with several road signs pointing off in different directions. i chose the gay-lake linden turn at the junction, and the tall smokestack ruins of the old mohawk mining company stamp mill told me i was coming into the small village of gay. i briefly hiked the old cement foundations left from the stamping plant, trying to imagine what it was like during the boom years of the copper mining era.

passing the eastern shoreline of lake superior on my journey back to calumet, i noticed several large tri-level houses, with attached three-car garages. i wondered about the souce of money for the owners, if they had worked jobs in detroit and chicago polluting the environment for greedy gain, escaping to their retirement in the pollution free keweenaw peninsula.

i drove past one mansion where an older lady was sunning herself in a lawn chair in the front yard, near two new cars parked in the driveway. this forced me to wonder: should a person work most of his life only to possess an expensive house, fancy cars, and a collection of costly household belongings or were there other things more important.

i was certain that whoever t. kilgore splake might be, he would never ever trade his coffee-stained collection of poems in *soul whispers* for this keweenaw peninsula life style and estate.

finally back in calumet and driving down pine street i suddenly saw the sign "artis used book store." i stopped in the shop and introduced myself to stephanie ryalls. she owned the store with tom mckeever who also ran a computer-based book selling business from home. stephanie said i should make sure to visit the calumet theater, probably the best experience in learning the past history of calumet. i was pleased to discover that the artis bookstore inventory had a used paperback edition of vonnegut's *god bless you, mr. rosewater*. i was not extremely keen on paying the high collector's value for an original dell vonnegut publication.

i asked stephanie what she could tell me about the cliffs, which i understood were somewhere north of calumet. after a quick chuckle she told me i ought to talk with two bears and little hawk, the ed gray grandsons who were the proprietors of jikiwe's art gallery over on fifth street. she said that their father, ed, believed that the cliffs were a very special spiritual location. before leaving the artis used bookstore i told stephanie that it was too bad she did not have a copy of the "cliffs notes" for the herman hesse book *steppenwolf* which was next on my reading list.

it had been a long day for me, visiting places, meeting people, and doing a lot of serious thinking, and suddenly it was over. after dinner i turned off the motel lights, pulled the blanket up to my chin, and let the ghost of old morpheus lead me into the land of sweet zzzzz's.

the next morning before opening my eyes i could hear the light wet drops of what would be an all-day soaking of precipitation. i decided to move more slowly, getting coffee and breakfast at john's family restaurant, a block from the elms motel on fifth street. then i returned to my room to read the splake chapbook manuscript "beyond ashes – a becoming."

beyond ashes

a becoming

escaping battle creek
first week in may
on vacation
until september labor day

forgetting lectures and classrooms
kellogg community college
north of mackinaw bridge
michigan's upper peninsula
pictured rocks outback
adams trail primitive wilderness
between munising and grand marais
relaxed daily diet
with trout fishing odysseys
cold pabst sixer
sharp cheddar wedge
alger county topographic maps
bronco passenger seat
seeking new beaver dams
trout fishing in america
rainbow fillets bacon potatoes
frying pan dinner feasts
one summer reading vonnegut
kurt's dell publishing titles
sirens of titan
player piano and mother night
god bless you mr. rosewater
welcome to the monkey house
slaughter house five and cat's cradle
breakfast of champions
meeting kilgore trout
quiet reclusive author
noting his literary works
barring-gaffner of bagnialto
the pan-galactic memory bank
early one morning
ross lake road camp
hacky-doodle breakfast table
coleman stove hot coffee
naggy early hangover

warming body by
last night's fire embers
reflecting past few days
catching sullivan creek trout
full creel limit
seeing sandhill cranes
gemini lake shallow swamp
kicking up black bear
grocery and mail trip
melstrand store visit
scribbling words
green mead 4x6 memo book
writing a poem
enjoying the creative rush
next day
writing three or four more
adding additional rough drafts
fall semester
back on college campus
still writing poems
scared of future failure
choosing a pen name
something to hide behind
if my writing stunk
borrowing vonnegut's trout
becoming t. kilgore splake
splake a northern planter trout
finding my first chapbook
kellogg community college bookstore
detroit lady's poetry
for a dollar fifty cents
putting together my summer poems
publishing *pictured rocks memories*
t. kilgore splake collection
feeling quiet satisfaction

suddenly realizing
"i want to write"
long battle creek nights
drinking and praying
"please give me the chance
to see where poetry might take me"
surprise early retirement
fleeing battle creek
moving to mun-i-sing
upper peninsula bardic exile
living like a hermit
small west end old house
defying other faculty voices
those left behind on campus
their concerns
"all that free time"
"what about upper peninsula winters"
reinventing my life
learning to become a poet
feeling evening sadness
when i'd lost another day
loving season of long white
with fewer distractions
thrilling upper peninsula storms
ice snow rain thunder lightning
often trees bending in dangerous winds
pink and green autumn auroras
writing daily
learning poetry by doing
not reading others ideas
discovering my "self"
like norman mailer's
advertisements for myself
literary journal reflections
solitary wordsmith

as ghost of dylan thomas
in his irish shed
writing exciting words
"do not go gentle into that good night,
old age should burn and rave at close of day;
rage, rage against the dying of the light"
finishing munising nights
npr classical music
crushed beer cans in sink
half-finished new poem
rattling brain skull cavity
dreaming like annie
loud mouth red-haired orphan
"tomorrow tomorrow tomorrow"
after four or five years
finally developing my voice
at last free from
hemingway brautigan carruth
william carlos williams jim harrison
their words and sounds
t. kilgore splake now real
contesting his elusive
damn dame lady muse
new poems mind
understanding writing is not
disturbing old time cats
my poems must
"yelp" and "moan"
be free from
conventional literary demands
a rhythmic voice
that is honest
emotionally intense
unlike elia kazan
others who named "names"

huac members questioning
feeling certain a good person
can produce great art
a faithful trust
their writings
contain serious and solid
honest human conscience
december 17, 2004
younger sister mary passing on
albuquerque new mexico hospital
successful by-pass surgery
never regaining consciousness
three packs a day
unfiltered pall mall reds
"negra modelo" beers
still not a shabby life
mother margaret
older sister catherine
dying a few years earlier
leaving tom last smith blood
writing poem for betsy
asking myself
who were my parents
emery and margaret smith
what did my mom and dad believe
settling in michigan
abandoning manifest destiny
dreams of great lands
lying farther west
making three rivers home
community a reasonable place
family problems solvable
preserving american history
purple mountains majesty
amber fields of grain

acquiring material belongings
car house furniture fine clothes
smith dream world
never really challenged
personal morality ever tested
without addictive needs
or broken by separation
lost to bitter divorce
finally dying with
good opinions of themselves
margaret determined housewife
always dusting and sweeping
vacuum, a loud roar
keeping smith house spotless
mother deeply narcissistic
not really in outside world
important historical events and people
emery taught junior high school
on his way to selling insurance
never achieving any reputation
significant personal mark
fame others acknowledge
a celebrated leader
growing fear
becoming like dad
suffering fools gladly
proof only stupid are happy
yet family demands
becoming something professional
wear a new suit
white shirt and tie
not work in denim jeans
name sewed
in shirt pocket circle
successful pusher and mover

unlike richard burton
martin dysart role
equus psychiatrist
making others normal
passionate feelings for greece
"i'd like to live there"
like artist henry denander
aegean home on hydros
raising grapes
visiting "lulu"
island village's pet donkey
writing poems
painting pictures
dysart shouting
"that boy galloped"
"alan strang galloped"
while dysart never had
holding deep personal doubts
taking away alan's fears
surrendering his primitive feelings
making him normal again
to buy cars and motorcycles
monthly bank payments
weekends drinking booze
smoking dope and chasing girls
going to porno movies
alan strang martin dysart splake
slaves to "chinklechankle"
controlled by society's demands
splake-smith
taking college classes
passing semesters
doing well
in subjects that i liked
getting an university education

b.a. m.a. ph.d degrees
instead of
pressing wilderness edges
living on alaskan frontier
modern day "mountain man"
like old free trapper
dressed in buckskin
coonskin cap hawken rifle bowie knife
living on fish dried meat pemmican
wild-ass bearded ghost of
bridger colter kit carson
bill "old solitaire" williams
alan strang like gay langland
one of society's "misfits"
turning wild horses loose
wild desert freedom
to run fuck be free
away from today's
numbing dumbing existence
films books magazines
seventh-grade reading level
simple *reader's digests* summaries
people traveling everywhere
places to go and see
gasoline starved refugees
satisfy having been there
desperately trying to be happy
jock sport games
promoting happy group spirit
baseball football basketball
more needing more
television "nonsense"
media telling people what to think
censoring poets artists
in touch with human life

instead demanding nice
tapioca flavored desserts
younger boys and girls
without existential crisis
unable to be bored
demanding continuous laughter
daily fun and games
shopping dancing movies
summer beach sun tans
lacking drive and ambition
smoking dope for breakfast
hanging out all day
chilling with buzzed friends
others shaking and baking
"new meth" formula
smokin' snortin' injectin'
flying under radar
sophisticated ignorance
never realizing
they will grow old
need doctors and medicines
facilities for elderly care
margaret's narcissistic fever
giving me her attitude
"you are what you do"
necessary survival skills
emery's weak coronary
big muscle insufficiency
my dad's inheritance
splake enlarged aorta
arrhythmic beat pulsations
keeping me busy
having mri exams
frequent clinic visits
recent fall appointment

doctor marder checkup
upper peninsula cardiovascular office
marquette general cat scan
hospital an underground society
striped line corridors
taking me to radiology
basement "waiting room"
people waiting others' surgeries
time for their exams
television on weather channel
calm low volume
safe viewer format
bulletin board message
"we need blood"
"o+o and a+a important"
wife holding husband's hand
his grim threatened stare
true love indeed
i never had
or managed to piss away
feeling like hospital prisoner
desperately thinking
"air give me air"
"i want to go home now"
lady ahead of me
waiting her cat scan
on hospital gurney
tied to medical technology
lights flashing beeping noises
hoping to find cancer
surgically burn it out
large black man
wheelchair bound
stroke victim unable to speak
sitting alone at home

watching television shadows
staring at pastel wall
splake surely knowing
"no not me"
doctor marder saying
"nothing has changed
next appointment two years"
adding at my age
"surgery is a risk"
still taking care
a couple more years
decade maybe
rental car turning miles
houghton airport return
god's country bardic 'res'
continuing to live
without divine creator
no morphine narrative
seriously wondering
what did camus ever do
checking under kitchen sink
making sure
.357 blue-cross blue-shield
splake insurance policy
still beside the drain pipes
later embracing morpheus
drifting into nighttime slumber
thinking even old guys
still have passion
believe in thoughts of love
gray geezer
still living alone
fading sense of chivalry
opening car doors
helping with a coat

saying "thank you"
yet "match.com"
computer dating service
full of independent women
still needing preferential treatment
ladies with strong religious beliefs
hard moral prescriptions
defining rightness
narrowing personal growth
discouraging exciting adventures
also females
who don't read books
possess deep interior feelings
a basic human soul
babette's conglomerate café
breakfast and coffee drinking femmes
wearing sweatshirts
warner brothers disney
comic cartoon characters
also happy smiley faces
empty unexamined lives
with motor-mouth opinions
on things that do not matter
rear ends continually growing
fat fat fat
thinking a few years ago
distant affair with mary
younger steuban poet
girl who could
"talk the talk"
but not write seriously
sad "craig's listing" lady
looking for a great smile
someone to make her laugh
having a lot of fun

no tender affections
wanting another to love
recalling splake memoirs
the winter diary
1950's high school junior
declining three rivers vacation
deciding not to visit
younger sister mary
east tenth street
fifth-floor walkup apartment
pre "big apple"
new york city
missing *sixteen americans*
museum of modern art
rauschenberg jasper johns de kooning
new artists paintings
or discussing creative ideas
with pollock rothko franz kline
over cedar tavern beers
young tom not
walking through allan kaprow's
18 happenings in 6 parts
gallery room-size "action collages"
feeling inside
an artist's abstract painting
better appreciating charles kauffman's
serious literary ambition
directing *synecdoche new york*
movie of brutal realism
actors celebrating mundane existence
living out their lives
as passing society continues
like william shakespeare's quote
"all the world's a stage
men and women merely players"

abortive teenage decision
missing new york's
small art theater films
french "new wave" auteurs
bergman's *seventh seal*
polanski's *knife in the water*
antonioni's *l'aaventura*
european directors
pushing fresh cutting edge
movies influencing
coppola spielberg george lucas
works of peter bogdanovich
future sundance "indie" films
john cassavetes showing
movies could be made anywhere
his 1959 *shadows*
capturing beat generation alienation
proving cinematic excellence
comes from the artist
not hollywood studios
men with the money
solitary graybeard whatevers
luck fate odds
without any control
creating a new self
sometimes besting elusive muse
poet still writing
leaving a few words
with fox fire glow
a tiny spark
lighting forest blackness
yet artist quickly forgotten
like dave church
providence rhode island
taxi-cab bardster

recent thanksgiving morning
fatal heart attack
whose name i still scribble
each passing morning
on my agenda schedule
also drinking cup of green tea
in his memory
so very soon
rat bastard time will vanish
coming day for
dave engel
rudolph wisconsin author
scattering my dusty remains
cliffs green stone summit
joining jikiwe's great grandfather
"golden hawk"
his other native spirits
with copper mining ghosts
who bought their candles
at mining company store
climbing up and down
mine's slippery ladders
with son fishing
daughter picking thimbleberries
wife weeding garden
"the good life"
waiting at home

as i laid the pages of "beyond ashes – a becoming" on the
motel room nightstand i was struck by how splake's powerful
words were lingering inside me. i envied splake's escape from
college classes and spending his summers getting rid of his
teaching burn out. i was curious if a check of past kellogg
community college faculty members would reveal a smith on the
list of professors. in addition i mused if he would be located in

the english department or some other academic area not related to literature, even though he was quietly writing poems.

i pondered splake's summers of camping, trout fishing, reading, and writing the "magnum opus" first poem. in my mind's eye I could see how those experiences changed his thinking as well as the direction of his life. quietly i asked myself, what does a person who decides he wants to be an artist early in his life do in order to have the same creative epiphany that splake suddenly discovered that morning in his pictured rocks lake superior wilderness camp?

after rereading splake's long poem it was easy to see how he took kilgore trout, the character from kurt vonnegut's book *breakfast of champions* and became t. kilgore splake. i was interested in finding out what else splake had done in pursuit of achieving a modest recognition in american literary history.

the "beyond ashes" long poem also described the bardic exile in munising and the long days writing in order to discover his self, and develop his own original voice.

splake's writing described his mother and father as an ordinary housewife and insurance salesman who would have liked their son to grow up and become a doctor, lawyer, or make lots of money, but not become a poor struggling poet. it was interesting that the smith family ethic stressed being somebody and doing something important in life rather than merely lacking the ambition and drive that most other people in our society exhibit.

it seems like most young men in the 1950's, he chose to chase after the college diploma instead of heading north to alaska and discovering himself in the wilderness as a jeremiah johnson mountain man. the university campus and classes also caused him to miss making connections with his older sister mary and her artist friends in the bohemian greenwich village of the 50's.

the splake final years appear to be solitary ones, living alone, but not sounding lonely. he did not have a wife or significant girlfriend in his later years, probably because any possible women friends had only lived unexamined lives of their "same old same old" personal behaviors.

at the conclusion of "beyond ashes" it seems that for some reason the cliffs, the green rock elevation north of calumet, gave the poet a quiet place to retire to and meditate over the mysteries of human behavior.

i was thankful that the mother of kay-lee had e-mailed me the materials that provided a better understanding of splake. the next thing i had to do was find two bears and little hawk and see what jikiwe's art gallery had to offer. the noon menu at the conglomerate café suddenly seemed interesting, since my early breakfast was digested a long time ago. while waiting for the traffic to clear on sixth street i thought about the calumet theater, wondering if the building was open, remembering stephanie's recommendation to see what it looks like inside.

i had just stepped through the large double doors into the theater's foyer area when a voice said "good morning, i bet you're an early tourist season visitor that wants to check out the calumet theater." i met davey holmbo, the theater's artistic technical director who told me it was too early for the guided tours of the theater, but he would be glad to turn on the overhead lights so i could really see what the old theater was like. suddenly i was gazing in awe at the amazing oil paintings on the proscenium arch of the different creative muses for painting, drama, poetry, sculpture, and music. there were also front row box seats on the main floor with white ratan chairs for the theater patrons. the theater had three different levels but the upper balcony had not been used in recent years. i grabbed the third balcony handrail firmly as i took a long look at the theater's stage that seemed very far below. in the theater's lobby i found large portraits of the past greats of american theater hanging on the wall. among the stage stars of earlier times were sarah bernhardt, lillian russell, douglas fairbanks sr., and helena modjeska. davey told me that other actors and customers had claimed to have seen the ghost of helena modjeska in different parts of the calumet theater.

davey, as the theater's artistic director, working with limited finances, helped chose what actors and performances the theater could hire. it was not a mystery that the new rozsa center in houghton, with air-conditioning and easier handicapped access, could afford a higher class of performers and stage shows, considering the generous purse strings of michigan technological university.

davey told me i should stop next door at shute's bar and have the owner show me the red light in the back that used to blink in the old days to tell the theater customers that it was time for the next scene or act to start. davey also shared with me the old calumet wives tale that many people believe there is an old underground tunnel that connects shute's bar and the theater. after thanking davey for his generosity in showing me the theater, i left to find jikiwe's art gallery, but halfway down the block i paused and looked back at the old red lake superior sandstone building with creaks and helena modjeska's ghost. i felt for certain this is where splake would read his poetry, not with all of the pomp and splendor of the rozsa center in houghton.

at jikiwe's art gallery i learned that little hawk was the native name for justin gray, and his younger brother two bears was allan gray. after our greeting pleasantries i asked the two young men how they ever decided to move to calumet and become the curators of the art gallery that their grandfather started. it seems that when they were younger, each summer they would leave their detroit home and visit gramps. this meant putting aside their video games and computer programs for two weeks, for trout fishing with ed gray, jikiwe. ed was native american and belonged to the objibway tribe. several years earlier at a special indian ceremonial celebration he was given the native name of jikiwe. allan told me that every morning before they left to fish jikiwe would be in his studio writing in a large notebook. when asked what the writing was about, their jikiwe replied that it was a story for them to read later when they had grown up.

jikiwe passed over the same year that justin and allan graduated from high school, so besides their diplomas, they also possessed the memoirs of jikiwe. they told me that after reading the reflections from the memoirs that they suddenly realized how important the people and places in the keweenaw peninsula were and that they had to live here. trashing their video game addiction and the "hurry up and wait" lifestyle of the below the bridge flatlands, they moved to calumet and bought the building with jikiwe's art gallery in it.

when i mentioned that i would like very much to see and hike in the cliffs north of calumet, justin drew me a quick map showing the route to drive to the cliffs trail entrance. then allan told me, if it wasn't raining tomorrow morning, to meet me there at 10 o'clock and he would show me the old mine remains on the cliffs summit. i asked them "do you know anything about t. kilgore splake?" they both replied that jikiwe and splake had been very close friends. justin said his grandfather had published a book or two of splake's poetry. allan added that they used to hike and climb together to their special places in the cliffs. i thanked justin for the map and told allan, that short of a keweenaw peninsula monsoon, i would meet him tomorrow and be ready to hike and climb.

because of the time i spent with justin and allan the conglomerate café's noon-hour luncheon crowd had eaten and left. once again i felt i had my own personal restaurant for a quiet meal. the soup of the day was lentil-garlic-mushroom. feeling extremely hungry the bowl of warm nourishment tasted great. while walking out the front door, leah called after me, and said her sister lila had just graduated from gogebic community college with her nursing degree and might be interested in going out with me.

smiling, i just waved her off, but i was thinking, a date with lila, hmm. feeling thirsty i decided to stop at the u.p. pub for a fast beer before returning to herman hesse's book *steppenwolf.* in the bar i met "call me karl walser" who bought me another draft and told me he was up from the down river detroit area to put a memorial wreath on the grave of his grandmother and grandfather at lakeview cemetery in calumet. he told me that his grandfather was a copper miner and in his late 50's when the calumet-hecla mine shut down for good in 1968. the grandfather drew social security benefits and worked odd jobs around calumet, while karl iii's father moved down state to wyandotte, michigan to work at the pennsylvania chemical company and raise a family. so, my u.p. pub tall stool partner was back in his home town paying his family respects. patting karl on the back and thanking him for the cool suds kindess, i left the tavern thinking what a small world we live in. karl and i both visiting grandparents' graves.

back at my motel room, i spent the rest of the afternoon with harry haller, maria, hermine and the magic theater. i also thought a lot about luigi and carissima and their two kids in iron mountain. theresa had moved to houghton in 1926 to go to michigan technological university. she married her economics professor and they relocated in detroit somewhere. when the iron ore mines in iron mountain went belly up, young luigi moved to calumet in search of a new mining job. he somehow seemingly vanished, a mystery in the meneguzzo family history.

allan's old rusty pickup truck was already parked at the cliffs trailhead path when i arrived the next morning. we hitched our small rucksacks over our shoulders and started hiking down the cliffs trail. while crossing a small creek by stepping on the winter ice out log timbers, allan told me that he and justin had looked over the collection of materials their grandfather left behind. allan said they found an old chapbook, *betsy*, that they guessed was about t. kilgore splake's sister. they also discovered the rough draft of a manuscript titled "cliffs notes" that jikiwe and splake were probably working on to publish. allan said he would give me the writings after the hiking and climbing of the cliffs.

while trekking upward allan pointed out the old cobblestone smoke stack of the north american mine, which had been a companion to the cliffs mining operations. we also passed a water seep gushing forth fresh may rains in a steady stream. allan pointed out the twists and turns in the cliffs trail, explaining that if you made a wrong turn, instead of reaching the summit you would be hiking to eagle river or end up at five mile point on lake superior.

i asked allan "why did splake and jikiwe make frequent visits and hike to the summit of the cliffs?" allan replied that before the white settlers and miners moved into the cliffs, they were a place where his native ancestors had lived and they were sacred to him. jikiwe's great grandfather golden hawk had worked in the cliffs mines from the beginning in 1860 until his death there in 1883. for splake, the cliffs were most likely a special spiritual place he went to for his periodic existential renewal.

upon reaching the summit we viewed another old cobblestone chimney, and huge piles of poor rock tailings from the cliffs copper mining activities. allan led me through a short path in the woods and showed me the major shaft for the cliffs mining. at the height of the cliffs mining prosperity the shaft went down over 5,000 feet into the earth. after walking a few more steps we came to the cliffs escarpment overview. we paused to see the vast panorama of the northern keweenaw peninsula below us. allan pointed out an old birchbark tree and said it was splake's "poet tree" where he attached poems, postcards and small art works. the tree looked feeble but for trees to last and thrive in the keweenaw hard rock they had to be tough. allan shared with me that splake's ashes were scattered under the "poet tree" when he died.

our walk back down to the ground-zero beginning of the hike was quiet. allan pointed out a small trail heading away from our path and said "this is the way to splake's 'point betsy.'" he told me that splake used to tie a red tibetan prayer flag to an old pine bough at the cliffs edge to pay respects to his sister betsy. after we reached allan's pickup and my artful dodger, i got the *betsy* chapbook and "cliffs notes" pages. allan returned to calumet and his art gallery work while i decided to drive to eagle river to relax on the lake superior beach, read a few pages of *betsy* and think about splake and my day of climbing in the cliffs. i stopped at the phoenix store and got myself a cold quart of blatz, wondering if i might see a lake freighter near the lake superior shore. the cover of *betsy* had a fat little girl pedaling an old tricycle. a small boy, probably splake, was hanging onto her skirt. i quickly read a couple of the early pages of *betsy* and laid it down on a beach stone thinking i would read the rest later.

betsy

"lets play daniel boone"
mary declared to picnic friends
surprising other family parents
stale imaginations dulled
by orderly house beautiful demands
dreaming next
keeping up with joneses
expensive material possessions
home bulletin board gold stars
elementary middle grades
all-a report cards
high school salutatorian honors
girlhood comic book heroines
glamorous brenda starr
newspaper reporter
pursuing dangerous intrigue
basil saint john lover
mysterious black orchids
mary marvel wonder woman lois lane
strong women besting evil villains
"terry and the pirates" fan
adopting special nom de plume
"captain red hurricane smith"
flying squadron companion

now, i could understand "point betsy" and splake's red tibetan prayer flag symbol. he was simply honoring his memory of "captain red hurricane smith."

while driving back to calumet and my elms motel room sanctuary i thought well, i finally had a good idea of who the author of *soul whispers* was. t. kilgore splake who has become the forgotten poet of the upper peninsula. it was nice tom smith late in his life discovered his creative talent and like the short life of a butterfly shared his visions for those who read and think about serious things. it seems that while splake grew tired quickly, flitting here and there on wings growing thin and colorless, there was a new poet-butterfly somewhere waiting for its time to arrive.

the next upper peninsula mystery for me to focus on was the son of luigi meneguzzo, or maybe more accurately, the son or daughter of the son of luigi meneguzzo. the last information that i had is that he left iron mountain and came to calumet in 1929 to look for a job in the calumet copper mines and then seemingly vanished. i thought, maybe if i learned a little bit about the history of copper mining in the keweenaw peninsula, it would provide me with a clue as to what happened to the meneguzzo son.

i arrived back in my new "le metrops" home away from battle creek and caught stephanie cleaning out the artis used book store's espresso coffee making machine before closing the store and going home for the day. looking over her brewing machine i said "that is really a state of the art piece of technology, where are the whistles and bells on that coffee cooker?" i asked stephanie who was a good person that could tell me about the past history of copper mining in calumet and across the keweenaw peninsula. she replied that frank bascombe, a retired unitarian minister from marquette, would probably be the nearest and best source of information. otherwise i would have to drive down the big hill into lake linden and hope to find clarence monette at home. steph said that frank was a friendly guy and i could find him at the copper town usa museum early tomorrow morning. stephanie also showed me a book that she had earlier cataloged from a recent estate purchase, arthur thurner's *calumet copper and the people*, saying it was probably the best history of the village. i paid her the few extra dollars for the silver anniversary edition of *calumet copper and the people*, thinking it would give me something to read when i got back downstate to battle creek.

i stopped and grabbed a warm four-pack of lowenbrau black ale at bucko's party store on fifth street. i took a hot shower at the motel while jim's pizza delivered dinner to my room. i fell asleep immediately after turning the final page of hesse's *steppenwolf* and had visions of harry haller, and the magic theater for mad men only.

the next morning, frank bascombe must have been running late. i sat in the copper town museum's parking lot wondering how bruce clark was doing with *steppenwolf* and the rest of his hesse books in his pictured rocks lake superior camping retreat. my first impression of *steppenwolf* is that the book was written for all the college sophomores to be found in future universities. for a quick moment i thought the book should be called "run harry run," or, "dancing my way to hell." i also felt that maybe the reader could conclude after reading *steppenwolf* that it was all right to kill the one you love and fuck the person you didn't care about.

harry haller, hesse's central character was an aging man who believes he is part man and part "wolf of the russian steppes." haller is frightened over losing the refinement, order and logic of society while at the same time admiring the savage freedom, strength and dangerousness of his wolf-like feelings. at the book's conclusion hesse says the wise person must learn to laugh at the meaninglessness of life and the mess that the world is in. once this is achieved, hesse says, one's new life can emphasize the pursuit of knowledge and creation of new works of art.

the arrival of bascombe's small foreign car interrupted my thoughts about *steppenwolf*. quickly i told him about luigi meneguzzo, the missing-in-action son of the iron mountain mining father. frank told me the tons of keweenaw peninsula boom copper that brought financial riches to mostly eastern investors was done and over with. the "old reliable" quincy mine in hancock had ceased work in 1949. after a copper miner's strike in 1968 the calumet and hecla company in calumet shut down their operations. then the champion mine north of calumet and the mine at white pine were operating for a few more years until they finally shut down. even if the price of copper would rise to a very high level, the cost and start up time in reopening the old mines was financially impossible. bascombe added that after years of being abandoned, the mines were flooded with billions of gallons of water and the supporting wooden mine timbers rotted from years of inactivity. frank whispered that any new serious thought about new mine starts would bring in the federal and state governmental environmentalists, who would demand that the mines be ecologically safe for the keweenaw soils. i realized that back during the turn of the century the mines brought freedom to the european immigrant, who were prevented from owning property, voting, and faced compulsory military service in their native country. but why would a young man today want to work hundreds of feet below where the sun never shines for a paycheck? before i left bascombe and the copper town museum, he strongly recommended that before going back to battle creek i should visit the old quincy number-two mine shaft headframe and hoisthouse, north of hancock. with my vacation almost over, and the time to head back to the kellogg company drawing near, i still decided to take a quick visit to the "old reliable" headframe and also see the quincy mining hoist. pulling into the parking lot, i met fred corbas, a quincy mine tour guide, who quickly showed me some of the significant features of the headframe structure. the intitial crushing of the ore was done inside the shaft house. there were two large steel bins, one for mass copper and the other for poor rock. the remaining stanchions were about 100 feet tall and supported the iron cables leading from the mining headframe to the quincy hoist house located down the hill behind the headframe structure.

the quincy mine drillings went 6,400 feet straight down. between 1852 and 1946 the copper ore mine paid an estimated $27,353.00 in dividend profits. fred pointed to the red brick walls of two other old buildings nearby, saying "that is what is left of the quincy blacksmith shop and the quincy machine shop." it seems that three or four years ago the roofs of both buildings caved in, leaving the machines and mining tools to rust. fred said the miner's "dry house" with lockers and showers had been destroyed from lack of attention over two years ago.

if there is a ninth wonder of the world my vote for that honor goes to the nordberg quincy hoist machinery. while standing in the hoist house looking at the massive hoist technology, i felt a quiet awe. as a small boy i was raised with tinker toys and erector sets, and thus, greatly appreciated the inventive engineering mind.

the horse power of the hoist could lower several skips of miners to their work sites below and also raise tons of copper ore at a fantastic operating speed. i climbed the spiral staircase, to the top of the quincy hoist, where there were two huge wheels with numbers on them to indicate the different levels of the quincy mine. for a brief moment i imagined that i was the hoist operator deftly moving miners and copper ore up and down the mine shaft. before leaving the quincy number two headframe site, i checked out the two old steam engines and tenders sitting on rails behind the quincy hoist house. climbing up into the cab on one of the engines, i grasped the throttle and briefly pretended that i was moving copper ore down the quincy hill to the copper smelter on the portage canal.

once i got back to calumet, feeling the need for a late lunch, i stopped back at the conglomerate café to check out the noon menu. a new good looking waitress met me and handed me a note, saying, "justin from jikiwe's art gallery asked me to give this to you." i thanked the young lady, ordered a reuben sandwich, and asked her if she was leah's sister lila. she replied that yes she was. she was working at the conglomerate until she got a nursing job at the keweenaw hospital in calumet or the portage view hospital in hancock. while lila was making and toasting my rye, corned beef, swiss cheese and sauerkraut afternoon meal, i quickly read justin's note:

splake,

allan learned from one of jikiwe's old friends that

splake has a monument in the calvary cemetery on the
five mile road north of ahmeek. calvary cemetery is an
interesting place, and i think you ought to visit it. sorry
i couldn't tell you this in person, but, allan and i are in
marquette today chasing an artistic adventure.

when lila returned with my sandwich i said, "it isn't busy right
now, why don't you sit at my table and tell me about the gogebic
community college nursing program." lila got a cup of green tea,
sat across from me and said, "whew, i thought that i would never
pass algebra and finally get my two-year diploma." she told me
she had received some tutoring in algebra from an old retired
ironwood math teacher, pat o'neill, and just barely passed the
course.
  i asked lila what she wanted to do now with her education and
life, and she replied, "well, i don't plan to be in nursing for the
rest of my life, but right now i just do not have any ideas of what
to do, except save some money." i learned that she wanted to stay
in the keweenaw peninsula area because she liked skiing. maybe
she would buy a house when she saved some money. someone had
told her that tom and stephanie were thinking about selling their
artis used bookstore, which she would be interested in.
  i told lila i really would like to have a date with her, but, right
now my vacation had simply run out of time. lila replied, "the
memorial day holiday is coming pretty soon. if you drive back
to calumet, we could go to my family's picnic celebration at the
beach in eagle harbor." i got lila's mailing address, phone number,
and e-mail connection and told her i would let her know about the
memorial day date very soon.
  after the conglomerate afternoon meal i drove north through
centennial, kersarge, and ahmeek. i found the calvary cemetery
on the sand point highway to eagle river. having no idea what to
expect, i found the cemetery unlike any other i had seen before.
most of my cemetery memories were of a somber location with
dreary monuments and mausoleums of rich people trying to buy

their way into heaven. calvary cemetery seemed designed to celebrate the lives of those buried there. i found plaster casts of angels and deer in all different sizes and dimensions. one grave even had a large black dog statue wearing a "welcome" sign around its neck. i discovered crushed white stone patios with lawn gliders and wooden benches for the visitors. there was another grave site with a white picket fence around it and a sign that read "garden of eden." the late afternoon breeze ruffled different prayer flags and religious tapestries. wind chimes were playing a soft cheery melody. i found a headstone with a cabin on a lake and a fisherman in a boat, and the statement on the monument said "let time go by – let suns rise – and i'll still be here." i also found a monument for jackson "hair bear" harry which had the full length of a lake freighter on it to recall the fellow's life time spent working on the great lakes.

finally i found the monument with "splake" carved in dark black letters on its front. after checking out his calvary cemetery neighbors, i discovered he was in the good company of "aunt holi," "signe ryti," "uhro bedladradich," "reyno haataja," and "hulda siljnan." i took out the pages of splake's "cliffs notes," the unpublished manuscript that he left behind with jikiwe. leaning against his granite stone i read the "cliffs notes" poem:

cliffs notes

young sixteen-year old face
trapped in graybeard body
early morning bathroom mirror
seventy-three years and counting
wrapping treadmill
minutes and miles
running to eagle river
back home to bardic 'res'
passing through phoenix loc
checking wrist monitor

blood pressure in 120's
pulse rate at mid-60's
now on first dawn hike
climbing cliffs
checking red tibetan prayer flag
flying at point betsy
sister mary elizabeth memorial
snow still covering
pebbles and small stones
remembering musical ballad of
david de los angeles
three fingered gypsy
refrains of "clifton mine"

"come all ye old miners
up from the deep
talk about the underworld
and secrets you would keep
come all ye old miners
from where the sun doesn't shine—
two miles underground
in the clifton mine
bring me a copper kettle
won't you bring me a silver dime
bring me precious metal
from the clifton mine"

trekking odyssey
in dim first light
hoping to renew
splake-smith spirits
fresh rush of energy
sharpening critical focus
footsteps crunching
rare frosty silence

lake superior winds calm
remaining withered leaves
quiet on bare tree branches
soon fog horn
will be sounding
five mile point lighthouse
warnings for lake superior
ore freighters
rocky seep thawing
frigid clear pool
sounds of new spring stream
drip drip dripping
thinking of t.s. eliot
his
the waste land verse

"april is the cruelest month, breeding
lilacs out of the dead land, mixing
memory and desire, stirring
dull roots with spring rain"

often alone
lost in cliffs silence
recalling musical sounds
public radio 90
marquette michigan
northern michigan university campus
stan wright's weekly
"classics by request"
modest mussorgsky's
"pictures at an exhibition"
rich full brass
pulsing strings
pealing bells and triumphant cymbals
carl orff's "carmina burana"

soft poetic tenderness
later exuberant
driving sarcastic edge
"in the tavern"
raucous drinking ballad
dark munich beerhall shadows
quiet days listening
munising "little house"
westend bardic voyeur
moving window to window
knowing all walnut street events
buying chalk
ben franklin thrift store
for kids drawing new art
on sidewalk squares
ten year long semester
discovering creative works
something you disappear in
learning to write poetry
by reading others
facing down blank pages
doing contest with
elusive damn dame lady muse
not curious about
james joyce's breakfast
when he wrote page 188
of *finnegan's wake*
avoiding writing workshops
different personality conflicts
concerned with safe salable stories
no *moby dick or gravity's rainbow*
coming from literary mix
finding my voice
without mfa degree
understanding hemingway's paris wisdom

write straight and true
munising nights
drinking cheap "old milwaukee"
waiting for mother to die
margaret's small estate
tommy's modest inheritance
providing financial buffer
new pickup truck maybe
early next mornings
collecting empty beer cans
stashed in kitchen sink
listening to vicky crystal
ispheming country and western station
learning to love
"your cheatin' this
and lying that"
honest american prose poetry
music setting tone
for "fuck it"
new basic bardic
long day "doin' it"
now old mining house
calumet tamarack location
where line is drawn
making my last stand
all of this
like strange distant dream
something that happened
another lifetime ago
crockpot madness stew cooling
crossword puzzles waiting
thinking of three rivers
dunkel elm east streets
smith family homes
remembering christmas celebrations

shiny tinsel icicles
warm kubrick-like
colored holiday lights
wrapped presents waiting
underneath decorated tree
each new spring
making orange-crate racer
flat old wagon bed
building fires also important
playing with sister's dolls
hours reading cooking book recipes
going to sunday school
summer church studies
tommy and stuffed panda
riding with dad
meeting new people
father selling more insurance
earning a decent living
high school diploma years passing
class reunions never attended
home town old friends
minds stopped working at puberty
age thirteen or shortly after
girls monthly period odors
boys madly jacking off
classes force feedings
solid american beliefs
becoming and staying popular
most important thing
white bread 1950's
graduating into predictable existence
marry settle down have kids
making babies not creative art
no paintings poems photographs
life career job

not doing what one wanted
never understanding
"who i really am"
numbing salary paychecks
spent in mall-mart stores
new stuff heavens
mad conspicuous consumption
accumulated adult "toys"
tri-level basements and garages
suburban middle-class houses
latest model tranny style
with vacation condos
fancy motorhome touristings
constant cell-phone conversations
providing new definition of
nada mas nada mas
huge plasma t.v. watching
poker card games
fishing and golf
miscellaneous espn jock sports
never asking
"is this all there is"
wondering about "carnauba"
next car wash visit
semesters classes students
kellogg community college tenure
teaching political science in coldwater
extra child-support dollars
barely surviving winter blizzards
driving back to battle creek
meeting third wife olga
american government lectures
lakeview high school nights
unused faculty sick pay
down payment for munising home

through passing time
two kcc students staying close friends
bruce holcomb and mike fitzgibbon
keeping regular contact
bruce gifting me
man in wire cage
original creative sculpture
another summer
helping me with a new roof
hot humid july days
nailing down asphalt shingles
munising little house
sharing his tales
motorcycle riding through southwest
artist friend in arizona
in self-contained home
musical buddy
handling hard times in n'awlins
describing six month stay
vienna austria artist hostel
traveling alone
to other european places
always visiting calumet
when i am seriously writing
following mike's adventures
fishing for ocean crabs
gulf of alaska trawler
adak and unalaska mailing addresses
letters from honduras
mike helping poor farmers
also driving ann arbor taxi
while getting michigan diploma
majoring in journalism
philosophy minor
taking mike's letters

writing *alaskan letters* chapbook
using his cab tales
in *ann arbor connections* book
yet always wondering
"why me" connection
maybe like jack
their always "on the road"
questing unknown places
trying to find america
then like sal paradise
hurrying home to "memere"
bruce now teaching algebra
kalamazoo special school students
make with "bia"
making timber harvest decisions
ashland wisconsin base
neither new poet tree caretakers
cliffs green copper summit
maybe someday
one will choose
to write a new
great american memoir
splake-smith not believing
in unlived lives
important to take risks
chasing wild-ass dreams
knowing there is something else
changing growing learning
visiting rockford Illinois
during munising days
hoping to connect
with *kumquat meringue* editor
christian nelson and splake
new chapbook title
also see "notzke"

los angeles california
poet and playwrite
woman i cared deeply about
ford tranny travel menu
cold crockpot potatoes
tab cola and faststop coffees
turning off wisconsin interstate
exiting north of fond du lac
weary of insane ugliness
urban metro sameness
slowing mph
window rolled down
breathing fresh rich aromas
new farm field fertilizers
finding christian
in swedish memorial hospital
chest pains possible heart problem
staying overnight for observation
talking with notzke
hospital basement cafeteria
my bardic skull cavity
full of mad "outta here" panic
discussing our painful separation
she a "city cat"
needing lalaland glitz and glamour
go go life style
splake unable to handle
small backwater redneck prejudices
nasty racial remarks
living with a black artist in calumet
notzke hummed in my ear
"take these tom"
pressing two soul rings
deep into my palms
hugging and kissing in the elevator

"notz" crying out
"i love you very much
please don't leave me"
soon tranny-tripping
turning highway miles
interstate tunnel-vision hours
back to god's country
munising "little house"
warm feelings of
"i live here"
thinking brother brautigan
got it right in his poem
"love is not the way
to treat a friend"
wild places have provided peace
summers in the pictured rocks
between munising and grand marais
somehow making monthly
land contract pays
owning 10-acre camp
point well and outside privy
ross lake road summer home
paying battle creek girl
airport bar waitress
to drive an old chevy van
across the mackinaw bridge
giving me a warm place
to think and sleep
van girl susie and splake
smoking breakfast dope
making love
drinking bottle or two of champagne
making love again
somehow baking "weed brownies"
in tin foil

on coleman camp stove
often thinking
while wrestling naked
sue and i
were like alonzo hagen's
"trout fishing in america" diary
each toke
slug of icy brut
trippy chocolate square
was another fishing trip
with more trout lost
sue's pictured rocks odyssey over
putting her on a gray dog
munising greyhound bus stop
later learning
after st. ignace stop
she got a job
waitressing and cleaning
at huron bay hotel
alone again
hiking and fishing
occasional beer at club majestic
talking alger area history
with fernedes and genevieve
one upper peninsula summer
reading all kurt vonnegut's books
another battle creek respite
finished herman hesse's writings
except *magister ludi*
the glass bead game
time when paperbacks
were cheap
returned to kellogg community college
september campus classes
later retiring

moving to live in munising
repaying my
upper peninsula debt
writing and publishing
soul whispers
poems and photographs
of pictured rocks memories
recently i fell in love
with a beautiful younger woman
mary thirty years old
with master's degree in english
northern michigan university
splake caring more
for her young daughter kay lee
buying her fall clothes
junior and senior school years
mary told me
she was raped at age thirteen
leaving me wondering
was she without a heart
unable to say "i love you"
to another man
her accumulated personal problems
with generation x
lack of determination
no inner drive or desire
caused the difficult pain
of breaking off our relationship
yet still googling kay lee
checking her artistic works
seeing if she has
new play to direct
starring in some performance
surveying my twilight moment
creative poems stories books

soon all will be gone
like ancient "clifton mine" remains
vanished and quickly forgotten
except for a few foundation stones
proof to curious hiker
we enter our world
alone and screaming
leaving the world
also quietly and alone
soon splake will join
moss-covered tombstones
"clifton mine" cemetery ghostly spirits
yet graying tommy
blacksheep of the smith family
often remembers the words in betsy
chapbook honoring my sister
"who were those people
father emery and mother margaret"
parents who never explained life
talked about important things
while we were growing up
with mary
we learned by ourselves
discussing sex secrets
with close friends
seeing movies and reading books
yet we chased adventures
unlike today's hovering possessive
helicopter moms and dads
children parental prisoners
without freedom to explore
there would be no jules verne excitement
star wars super fantasies
future literature dull
lacking original imagination

mother and dad would
never understand my tattoos
exotic body art
revealing important feelings
or appreciate my "motorcycle fevers"
one of earth's greatest joys
growling powerful cc's
rev rev revving chaotically
wildly rattling and shaking precious cojones
learning bike breakdowns a habit
of robert pirzig tale
zen and the art of motorcycle maintenance
realizing if you want predictability
buy a toyota camry
bikers able to debate
smooth aesthetic designs
honda "rice burners"
verus british artistic finesse
unable to remember
last time dad
hugged or kissed me
let me hold his hand
sad doggedness ww-ii masculinity
he had his job
basement or garage
massive collection of hardware tools
becoming a poet
would have disappointed emery
who wanted a son
to fulfill his unrealized ambitions
graduate with college degree
become happily married
giving dad a grandchild or three
wearing a dead pecker suit
selling insurance or real estate

boring bland good work
new model buick tranny
neighborhood status symbol
not chasing a creative itch
writing another poem
tommy-splake-smith
a mama's boy
with two older sisters
growing up like an only child
free to invent my "self"
margaret terrified
by germs and bacteria
being safe and clean
maybe obsessive-compulsive disorder
with possible bi-polar depression
at least serious pms
mother giving away my bubblegum cards
to methodist church rummage sale
st lou brownie pitcher
nelson potter
old new york giant outfielder
sid gordon
chicago cub shortstop
wayne terwilliger
my sports card collection
worth a small fortune today
still possessing memories of mother
rolling pin
huge yellow ceramic bowl
large mixing dish
for margaret's christmas recipes
cookies pies cakes
mom's turquoise china lamp
with torn and battered shade
still lighting my bardic corner

on early mornings
graying trout dancer
chasing the elusive muse
believing michael chabon right
statement in
manhood for amateurs
both of us
not giving a fuck
what other people think and say
splake wearing yesterday's clothes
deciding not to shower
rarely leaning clipper blades
against the bushy beard
taking a fast running piss
in bard 'res' kitchen sink
no more radio sounds
distant noise
enemy of creativity
yet feeling brain-skull ripple
when musical "oldie"
favorite song from the past
comfortable with my identity
splake working literary habits
unconventional writing style
like poet rascal edward estlin
e.e. cummings once wrote

"since feeling is first
who pays any attention
to the syntax of things
will never kiss you"

recent e-mail message from jikiwe
kudos for not selling out
keeping true to yourself

borrowing from kipling
rudyard's powerful quote

"to be your own man is a hard
business. if you try it, you will be
lonely often, sometimes frightened.
but no price is too high to pay for
the privilege of owning yourself."

ignoring babette's regulars
conglomerate café
morning coffee customers
people who can not imagine
having wasted all their time
without having a life
idling wondering
what to do today
my refusal to die
after drinking and heart problems
no more whiskey courage
librium tranquilized help
splake can't stop living
deny today's breaths
working on new book
fresh poem or story to tell
calm quiet tamarack house
silent literary sanctuary
knowing art exciting and dangerous
the only path to truth
writing working discipline
often full of pain
maintaining focus
continuing creative rush
sad reflection
old t.s. was wrong

in *the waste land*
"burial of the dead" verse
april is not the cruelest month
breeding lilacs memory and desire
there is more wisdom
in davd de los angeles
"a little sugar" lyrics
yes poetry readers
"richard brautigan he is the cruelest month"
with splake poem
from *twilight long white*
munising little house bard 'res'
describing april morning
coming into spring

"staring in wonder, spring chinook turning
walnut street hill into raging, sluicing currents,
rock-filled brown river tides,

late march daffodil buds pushing soil aside,
grassy islands growing before retreating snow
bank edges,

april, furnace off, backdoor open, inviting
welcome warm sun rays, barefoot, toes tickling
in soft carpet shag"

splake graybeard poet
old man living too long alone
alive to witness
bask in one more
ice out
blood bath

planning on an early morning return to battle creek and my desk at the cereal company, i decided to have an early dinner at the michigan house. with only a few early customers, the owner, tim bies, told me that he was renovating the old bosch brewing company's bar and hotel that was built in 1905. besides the restaurant he now had a brewpub, the red jacket company, making "oatmeal coffee stout." he was also renting two rooms on the second floor of the building. i felt drawn to a fine oil-painting-mural on the wall behind the bar that showed a happy brew-filled picnic that was finished in 1906. i ordered the " big annie pasta" dinner, which turned out to be such a huge meal i almost could not finish it. the red jacket glass of stout was the perfect accompaniment to dinner. i skipped dessert and retired to blow some serious zzz's at my elms motel room.

i awakened very early, planning on chasing the white line highway miles back across the upper peninsula to my battle creek home. i figured if i made good time first dawn would be lighting the bay as i drove down the long steep hill into marquette. it was possible that i might get between marquette and munising before the morning's dawn would break over lake superior.

in order to get going quickly i took the short portland street exit from calumet to the highway south to hancock, the portage liftbridge, houghton and miles east. on portland i passed a small tavern that had the pink neon "luigi's" shining in the front window. this completely surprised me, as i never really thought about luigi meneguzzo's son working at any other job than mining copper or iron ore. of course, i did not have time to stop and ask the bartender serving the "last call" drinks if he was any relation to the iron mountain family.

remembering the early history i read in carissima's diary, the new italian workers in iron mountain were intelligent as well as ambitious people. many worked in the iron mines for a few years, saved their wages, and opened new business operations. many established taverns, barber shops, ran livery services or were tailors, and had wives that became dressmakers or ran ice cream parlors and candy stores.

the meneguzzo's had a neighbor, mikolay gentofanti, who had ten cents in his pocket when he first got to iron mountain, and after a couple of years, he was the owner of the peninsula granite and marble company. i thought that when i came back to calumet on my next visit, i would have to check on the grocery stores, beauty salons, beer company distributors and insurance agents to see if i could find any of luigi's iron mountain relatives.

enjoying the early morning i decided against having any radio noise in the artful dodger, at least until it got light outside or i stopped for a quick on the road breakfast.

yesterday i had enjoyed reading splake's "cliffs notes" manuscript, and while there were two or three places in the work that repeated his early writings, what the hell, it was his memoir, right? i thought about calling or e-mailing justin and allan at jikiwe's art gallery and finding out what their feelings were on publishing "cliffs notes." it would be a nice gesture to the forgotten upper peninsula poet, not to mention a money earner at sidewalk days or the summer heritage festival in calumet. certainly turning the old manuscript into a new book was a serious idea to consider for the future.

after my return to life in battle creek i still had the vonnegut *god bless you, mr. rosewater* to read. i had only browsed through the book's final pages and apparently kilgore trout convinces the wealthy mr. rosewater that "people can use all the uncritical love they can get." mr. rosewater agreed and said that the hatred of lesser human beings did not have to be a part of our human nature.

i thought of the lives of many people i had met during my brief vacation and time away from battle creek.

luigi meneguzzo, like a later son of italy, vince lombardi, chose to "run to daylight," in search of his personal success. he was not satisfied to work the family farm in italy with his brothers. he gambled on finding a better life in america and the freedom to do what he wanted.

then there was tom smith who became a poet and changed his name to t. kilgore splake. splake left his prestigious position of being a college professor with blue-ribbon fringe benefits to live in creative poverty, just to write poems. upon reflection, it almost seems like splake's life had already been planned in advance, escaping kellogg community college, living and writing in munising, moving on to calumet, and finding the cliffs in the keweenaw peninsula. i wondered could he have finally found the home that it seemed he had been searching for all of his life?

i added ward pratt, dave clark, munising's corktown bar tara and calumet's conglomerate café lila to the list of those not satisfied to be the same people for the rest of their lives. ward chasing the ghost of hemingway and trout around the schoolcraft county and grand marais streams and rivers. bruce clark communing with nature, reading books in the pictured rocks wilderness, and learning more about himself. tara saving dollars in order to attend northern michigan university to study art. lila skiing in the keweenaw peninsula mountains, on her way to maybe buying a used bookstore. after meeting the people in calumet and checking out the many other places in the keweenaw peninsula, i thought that the kellogg cereal company job in battle creek would become extremely pale or tame by comparison.

after copper was discovered in the keweenaw territory, the white adventurers and later miners took the lands away from jikiwe's ancestors. during the boom copper years the mining companies needed more workers and calumet became a virtural melting pot of different nationalities. there were new people who came from england, germany, france, finland, sweden, poland and other countries.

today, with the copper jobs and profits long gone, however, the people who remain in calumet and across the keweenaw peninsula still represent a solid cohesive community. thurner in his history of calumet said that in spite of the wide variety of differences, a blending of the keweenaw culture through intermarriages, business

96

associations, jobs, schools, and social activities had created a common bond of unity. he predicted that calumet would have a prosperous future because "when we know one another, we can live together more peacefully."

as the morning's sky slowly lightens on the eastern horizon, i muse about calumet, luigi's tavern, the conglomerate café and lila. i also wonder if the ghost of splake might welcome a new poet tree and cliffs caretaker. a new red tibetan prayer flag flying over point betsy also seemed like a fine idea. finally, i wondered how in the world does someone run a used bookstore in a place so far from civilization where the winter long white is always six foot high and rising.